pivot and slip

PIVOT
~ and ~
SLIP
by Lilah Suzanne

interlude
press

ISBN 13: 978-1-941530-03-0
Published by Interlude Press
http://interludepress.com

Book design by Lex Huffman
Cover Design by Buckeyegrrl Designs
Cover Artist/Illustrator: C.B. Messer

"Within our dreams and aspirations we
find our opportunities."

- Sugar Ray Leonard

To the fandom that gave me my dreams back,
this book is for you.

Prologue

The left hook felt wrong from the moment he twisted forward: too wide and too high, leaving him open to the quick jab that landed on his temple. His head snapped back, teeth clacking closed, pain blooming as though an earthquake had cracked through his skull. The ring and surrounding area started to shift and spin, so Felix allowed his opponent to crowd him up against the ropes and curled his head in chin to chest, seeking refuge behind his gloved hands just to get his bearings until the ref stepped in and broke them up.

He collapsed into the metal folding chair in his corner, and a squirt of warm water hit his cheek and ear and dribbled down his neck. Head tipped back, aware of the clock counting down, Felix squinted at the crowd, a blurred and shimmering mirage screaming for their gladiators, screaming for glory. Screaming for blood.

Felix wobbled back into position with a shove from hands anxious for his win. The urgent instructions from his trainer reached him as if they were being shouted from underwater: muffled and muddled and dull, and the cheering crowd was soon drowned out by the deafening ringing in his ears. Felix shook his pounding head roughly, tapped his gloved hands together and bounced from foot to foot. This was his title he was defending. No way was he going down so easily.

He played defensively for a while, ducking, bobbing, his coiled reflexes like a snake stalking its prey, just waiting for the right moment. His opponent got him against the ropes again with hit after hit after hit until Felix could hear nothing but the sickening crunch of fist against bone, could see nothing but red. Rage coursed through his every vein. He was a trapped animal, desperate, wild. He didn't think, just moved.

He ducked, then pounced in a quick, powerful cross to the chin. It hit perfectly, even though Felix's balance was off, even though it burned white-hot through his shoulder and crunched across his knuckles as bile climbed his throat. He'd worry about that later. After he won.

The ground lurched and swayed beneath him as he wove to block another jab, but his limbs were heavy and slow, and it was too late. He had just enough time to see the world fade to black at the edges of his swimming vision before hitting the floor face first, the ref counting down as his world slipped and spiraled and tumbled from his grasp.

Then everything was gone.

Lilah Suzanne

Chapter One

Jack hummed softly to himself as he changed; a group of tourists on the subway had been loudly singing that damnably catchy 10,000 Maniacs song, and he had just resigned himself to having mid-nineties alterna-pop stuck in his head for all eternity. He folded his street clothes neatly and set them in a pile on the top shelf of his locker with his shower shoes lined up in the bottom, gym bag hung from the hook.

His spot was prime real estate, tucked into the far corner behind the showers, away from the main changing area. He was usually the only person back there, especially on Tuesdays and Thursdays, his Yoga for Seniors days. He could hear his students over the spray of the showers, discussing the upcoming Yankee season, ribbing the few Mets fans.

Jack had found that he needed a few moments of solitude before launching into teacher mode, and the fact that his spot smelled mostly like shampoo and Old Spice didn't hurt. It sure beat the *eau de body odor* that permeated the rest of the locker room.

"Hey, Jack! There you are! Have I told you about my granddaughter yet? She's an accountant, very smart. And nice, wide childbearing hips!"

Jack tried his best to not grimace and turned around with a plastered-on smile. He shut his locker door with a satisfying clink of metal on metal and spun the dial on the lock, then smoothed down the curling edges of the masking tape on which *J. Douglas* was printed in fading ink.

It would seem his perpetual singleness was pathetic enough that now even his octogenarian pupils were picking up on it. This was the sixth time in the last few weeks that he'd been told about someone's granddaughter or great-niece or, once, a recently widowed friend.

This time the matchmaker was Mr. Silverstein, a small, stooped man with a softly protruding belly and large ears and a penchant for telling dirty jokes during class.

"That's very sweet of you, Murray, really. But I very much doubt that she's my type," Jack said politely. He'd quickly learned that getting right to the point was the only way to shake them off.

Murray's face fell. He scratched at his mostly bald head, then grinned and snapped his fingers. "Howard's grandson! Howie! Isn't he an interior designer?"

Murray shuffled off to find Howard and hopefully some clothes. Why did all of these conversations seem to happen with the other party sans clothing? To be fair, the locker room was just brimming with naked old men more often than not.

Jack called out a quick "See you in class!" and made his blessed escape. He was perfectly capable of finding dates on his own. An interior designer. Honestly.

He had to set up before class started anyway. And spend some time visualizing the sunset or a flower garden or really just about anything to push away the mental images lingering from the locker room. But when Jack got to the studio room and flicked the lights on, he was surprised to see someone already there, standing in the middle of the room as if he was lost.

"Um, hello. This is Senior Yoga. If you're looking for the weight training class, it meets in studio four downstairs."

He was certainly not a senior citizen. Jack guessed the man was about his own age, and he didn't really look like any yoga student Jack had ever worked with. He was shorter than Jack by a few inches but stockier, solid, whereas Jack had long been plagued by a lanky, sharp-boned frame and long arms that were only useful for swimming strokes and reaching soup cans on high shelves.

Jack took in the man's tawny golden skin over thick, rounded shoulders and arms well defined by the hard bulge of biceps and triceps. His black hair was trimmed short at the back and sides and thick on top, his face shadowed with dark stubble that would likely take Jack a week to grow out and would only end up looking as if he had buff-blond sand stuck to his cheeks and chin and upper lip.

The stranger began to speak and then looked away. His profile was strongly jawed and ruggedly handsome, and Jack was immediately attracted to him.

Jack slipped off his shoes and crossed the room, lifting a stack of mats to start spreading them over the gleaming hardwood. From the corner of his eye he could see the man's reflection in the mirror that covered the back wall as he shifted anxiously and rubbed at the back of his neck before picking up a purple mat for himself.

"I know. There was some kind of mix-up, or I did something wrong when I registered? But I was already here and the lady at the front desk said it was okay... No, it's weird. I should go. I don't know what I'm doing here."

Jack dropped the stack of mats onto the floor with a thud and stepped over to stop him, surprised at his own desire to keep this guy around a little longer.

"No, don't," Jack blurted, and his breath caught. Not only was the guy gorgeous, but this close up Jack could see the lingering evidence of some recent injuries: a yellowing bruise under one eye, a bandage wrapped around his left hand and an angry scar stretching across one temple and disappearing under a thicket of black hair.

"I—I mean, you paid for it, right? May as well get your money's worth. I don't mind a little fresh meat," Jack squeezed his eyes shut. "I mean, young meat. I mean. Oh God."

Maybe Handsome Stranger would be better off leaving after all. Clearly Jack wasn't fit to be in close proximity to men on his own, let alone date them.

But the guy smiled warmly and Jack's stomach swooped. He was cute when he didn't look as if he was two seconds away from punching a hole in the wall. "Yeah. May as well."

The rest of the class started to trickle in then, and Jack heaved the mats off the floor so he could finish setting them out.

"I'm Felix."

"Jack Douglas. And I'll be your fumbling, awkward yoga instructor today," Jack gave a little curtsy, mats spilling from his arms.

"Besides, maybe you came here for a reason, Felix. Sometimes our mistakes lead us to our destinies."

Jack could feel Felix's eyes track him as he finished setting up, then stood in front of the class gathered around the room sitting cross-legged on their rainbow-hued mats. Jack expected Felix to catch on and follow their lead, like most new students, but he just stood on his mat, jaw clenched, hands curled into fists.

Just as Jack started the guided meditation to begin the session, Felix stalked across the room to the door, flung it open and slammed it behind him with an echoing bang.

Chapter Two

The abrupt storm-out had left Jack off-kilter and unable to focus for the duration of his class. He'd even botched his tree pose demonstration, which he could otherwise do half asleep, and was then forced to brush off several concerned grandmotherly queries and a somewhat worrying, exaggerated wink from Murray.

Now he scowled and stabbed his finger at the computer keyboard behind the front desk, looking for this Felix (Felix Montero, aha!) so he could contact him and inform him how unimpressive his little show was.

"If you break that computer, you know management won't get us another one. I think they had to time travel to find that dinosaur as it is." Sitting on the very edge of the chair next to his, Lydia frowned as she shuffled through some forms and secured them to her clipboard.

"Sorry," he grumbled, waving in a member with a glance at her card. "There was an... incident."

"A cute guy incident?" Lydia asked with a waggle of her eyebrows. She looked as frazzled as usual, her brown hair twisted into a bun and secured with two Bic pens, the collar of her shirt half up and one pant leg bunched at the ankle.

"Why do you always assume it's a cute guy?" Jack snapped. He reached over to fix her shirt, and she patted his cheek before standing with a spin of her chair.

"Because I sent him to you." She scooted around the desk as Jack switched his scowling directly to Lydia. "He's super hot—don't give up!"

Jack tossed a towel after her from the stack of clean ones they kept at the front desk. "Worry about your budget meeting and quit meddling!" he called to her quickly retreating back.

"I'll see you at home!" she called back with an air kiss, and disappeared around the corner.

Jack hesitated, his finger hovering over the escape key. Then, biting his lip, he finally typed the numbers into his phone, feeling just a little ridiculous now that the initial annoyance was wearing off.

Felix had seemed so nice and cute and adorably flustered at the start of class. Sure, there was this edge to him. But Jack had made him smile. And Jack could admit that he wanted to see if he could do it again. And again.

Slumping forward in the chair, he sighed and rested his head wearily on his hand. That kind of anger usually came from internalized pain. Jack knew what that felt like all too well. Wasn't that why he became captivated by yoga in the first place—because it was a way to release that toxic energy and stress?

He pressed the off button on his phone until Felix Montero's name and phone number faded away and tucked the phone back into his gym bag. As he climbed the stairway back to the studio to begin setting up for his advanced class, Jack felt a heavy tug of concern. Maybe he would just call Felix to see if he'd be willing to give the class one more try. Reach out to him as a concerned teacher. That's all. It had nothing to do with his biceps. Not even a little bit.

But when he rounded the corner and passed by the main workout area, he caught a flash of flying fists and a punching bag swinging heavily from its chain. Drawn in by curiosity and concern and some other force that seemed to propel him closer and closer, Jack watched as Felix twisted and punched and grunted. Everything about him was closed off and rigid. His arms were tucked in tight to his body, then shot out and back in sudden bursts of kinetic energy. His back was tense, his muscles were coiled and flexing, his shirt was pasted to his torso with sweat.

But it was his face that really brought Jack up short. Where he had looked wide-eyed and earnest

13

before that brief, shattering moment of frustration, he now looked dangerous and desperate, his eyebrows drawn low, eyes tightened to slits, nostrils flared. His jaw was clenched so tightly that Jack could see the tendons working as Felix ground his teeth.

And then Jack knew he was right. It wasn't anger. It was pain.

Felix grunted and swung, hitting the bag straight on and so hard that it scraped against the chain and twisted with a harsh screech of metal. He cursed loudly and tore the red glove off his fist using his teeth, then cradled it in his other, still-gloved hand with a hiss.

"Are you okay?" Jack crossed the room without thinking, moving into Felix's space. Felix glanced up briefly, but looked away and hunched his shoulders when he saw it was Jack.

"I'm fine."

Jack was close enough now to see his hand and hummed in agreement. "Oh yes, I'm sure your fingers always look that purple and swollen. Totally normal."

Felix whipped his head up and stared at Jack with narrowed eyes. Jack shifted uncomfortably, worried he'd provoked Felix further—but then Felix's body relaxed minutely, and he dropped his head low and huffed a laugh.

"Maybe it hurts a little," he admitted sheepishly. Felix lifted his arm to unstrap the other glove and then passed it across his brow to wipe away the rivulets of sweat. "I should, uh, get home. Put some ice on it."

"Oh no, I'll get some for you. Gym policy, follow me." Jack turned and started to head toward the tiny employee break room, hoping that Felix would follow him and not ask for any further clarification. It wasn't gym policy. Actually, it might have been. Jack had never really gotten around to reading the employee handbook, since when he started he thought teaching would be a temporary gig, just something to tide him over until he figured out what to do next. And yet, nearly two years later, here he was.

Jack dug around in the employee freezer—past the ice maker, a Lean Cuisine labeled "*KARA'S DO NOT EAT OR I WILL HUNT YOU DOWN I MEAN IT*" in thick black ink and the boxes of popsicles for the after-school kids—until he finally found an ice pack.

"Here we go," Jack said triumphantly, waving the blue gel pack around in front of him and closing the freezer door with his elbow. Felix accepted it with a quiet *Thank you* and sucked in a breath through his teeth with a wince. "So did the bag fight back or..."

Felix balanced the ice pack across his knuckles. "Actually, I broke a couple of bones about a month ago. Landed a punch wrong during a fight. Hitting the bag may not have been my best idea," he admitted, his eyes still focused intently on his hand.

"A fight? Like a bar brawl?" Jack sized him up.

He didn't look like the drunken bar fight type, despite the muscles, the odd storm-out and the furious beating he had just given the punching bag. Something about him seemed so sweet and kind.

"I'm a boxer," Felix said. Then his face twisted. "Or I was, anyway."

Something flashed across Felix's eyes, then, and Jack could see his jaw clamp tightly again, working and clenching. His breath came in shallow puffs through his flaring nostrils and he seemed visibly to be trying to calm himself.

Instinctively, Jack grasped Felix's free hand and stretched it across the distance between them to set it gently against his own abdomen. Jack could feel soft tremors shaking through Felix's fingers, the vibrations pulsing through Jack's T-shirt. Felix's eyes widened as Jack took a deep breath, filling his diaphragm and then his lungs and let it out steadily.

"Breathe," he instructed and inhaled again, nodding when Felix started to follow along. They breathed together, a slow circuit in and out and in, and Jack could see how Felix seemed to be calming bit by bit with every exhalation, his shoulders and neck loosening, his hand going lax and stretching wide across Jack's stomach from the bottom curve of his ribcage down to his belly button.

Jack focused on sending him a calming energy, passing it from his body into Felix's, until Felix's eyes blinked closed and his mouth parted, and then Jack found himself completely thrown off by the thickness of Felix's eyelashes and the plump curve of his mouth.

Jack's breath hitched on an inhalation, and Felix startled and opened his eyes, the ice pack falling to the ground with a soft thump. And when his hand flexed over Jack's stomach and he dropped his gaze to Jack's lips and back up, his eyes heavy-lidded and dark, the energy hummed and crackled between them.

"Douglas, I swear to God, if you ate my fiesta chicken I will castrate you."

Kara bustled into the break room, all swishing ponytail and hideous purple Lycra-blend workout clothes, pushing past Jack until he stumbled forward and his hip bumped into Felix's. Felix stepped back and pulled his hand away as if he'd been burned, and Jack had never wanted to brain someone with their own frozen convenience food as much as he did in that moment.

"Like I would ever eat congealed meat and flaccid vegetables in bland sauce—have we met?" Jack snarked, quickly recovering his wits.

Felix bent to pick up the ice pack from the floor, pressing his lips together against a grin. Kara ignored them and threw the frozen tray into the filthy microwave, grumbling under her breath as it slowly rotated and the timer ticked down.

"I should probably go," Felix said. He set the ice pack on the table and backed out the door.

Jack followed to stand against the door frame.

"Sorry about her. She's actually the best trainer here." Jack tipped his head in thought. "Probably because she's so evil."

"Well, that is one way to get results." Felix looked away, uninjured hand opening and closing at his side. "But I think I like your methods better. Thank you, by the way."

His eyes met Jack's, deep brown and rounded and so earnest that Jack's heart swelled with concern again. Why did he care about this guy so much? What was it about him that kept tugging at Jack right in his gut?

"Sure. Just—no hitting things for a while? If that punching bag pesters you again, you let me know and I'll take care of it for you. I got your back," Jack said, circling his hands into fists in front of him and mock-punching.

Felix smiled and ducked his head, turning away.

"You sure you're okay?"

Felix paused to look over his shoulder, sweaty and rumpled and so heartbreakingly sweet. "No, not really," he replied.

Chapter Three

"Okay, now move into cobra pose, remembering to go only as far as you feel comfortable."

Moving around the studio as he talked, Jack paused to straighten out a foot here, help widen shoulders there. "And breathe. In. Out."

A week after their first encounter, he'd been thrilled to see Felix shuffle in with the rest of the students—still looking shy and unsure, but there, with his hand seeming back to normal and the bruising under his eye barely visible. Jack hadn't been able to stop thinking about him, his mind circling wildly from chagrin to concern and to far less pure thoughts. Leading right back around to chagrin.

Instructing the class to transition into cat pose, Jack moved around the room, pressing his fingertips to stretched-out backs and giving his class reminders to exhale as they curved upward, while he made his way to Felix in the far corner. He danced out a hand to help him; Felix's body was too tight, too drawn and rigid. Then Felix saw him and drew in further and Jack wondered if he'd inadvertently crossed a line and made Felix uneasy.

It had been a revelation to him, when he'd first moved to New York from far-flung suburbia, that here he could socialize and mingle and interact without being treated as if he was contagious or only tolerated for what he could do, how often he won.

Then, at his first yoga class that Lydia had insisted they take together, he found touch to be guiding and careful and calm. A centering place he so desperately needed then.

Calling out for warrior pose, a more difficult one for some of his Tuesday and Thursday morning students, Jack approached Felix again cautiously, moving around him as slowly as if he were a startled foal.

"Hands flat," he said softly, ghosting his own open palm under the curl of Felix's to demonstrate. Not touching. Not quite. Felix puffed his cheeks and blew out a frustrated breath, stretching his fingers. Jack continued, soothing. "Keep your front foot straight and bend at the knee."

Felix's face knitted itself tightly into strained concentration as he tipped forward, arms spread, loose cut-off sweatpants sliding up his leg.

Jack had been so busy noticing the obvious muscles in Felix's upper body that he'd somehow completely missed the strength in his thighs. Jack swallowed and forced himself to focus.

"You're tipping forward too far. Try to focus on keeping your back straight."

Felix huffed and dropped his arms, that dark flash of anger distorting his features. "I'm awful at this. How am I the worst one in this class? It's pathetic."

"Hey, not all of us are deaf, you know!" Murray called from in front of them. Jack tried for a soothing smile as Felix stuttered an embarrassed apology.

"Ignore him," Jack said. He tipped his head and mock-whispered, "He'll be mostly deaf soon enough."

Felix's eyebrows shot up at Murray's indignant "I heard that!" and he finally cracked a grin when Jack sang back, "For no-ow."

Jack clapped his hands. "All right, go on to downward dog. Be aware of any lightheadedness, and Murray, let's try to keep our eyes on the mat and not on what Jan is doing in front of you, hmm?"

The class tittered, and Murray grumbled to himself. Jack walked around again, helping a few students into position, bracing hips as they bent over and stretched their hands out onto the ground.

Felix wobbled a little as he struggled to hold the pose, and Jack reached out to steady him but pulled back abruptly when Felix flinched away at his touch.

"I'm sorry. I keep making you uncomfortable."

"No. I—" Felix shook his head. He crouched on the mat, poking a finger into a small tear on the corner and refusing to meet Jack's eyes.

Jack was starting to worry that it was more than Felix just being uneasy with touch. That maybe Felix was uneasy with *him*. It had been a long time since someone had been that wary of him, that put off by something he had no control over, which was simply a part of who he was.

Ignoring the hollowed-out feeling in his stomach and the creeping echo of Jack from the past—guarded and closed off, keeping to himself at school and never getting close to any of his swimming teammates—Jack slipped between Felix and the wall next to him, asking the rest of the class to go ahead and relax into corpse pose.

"Try to copy what I'm doing."

Because, as much he wanted to stalk away and leave Felix to stew in his own discomfort and bigotry, he was a teacher—a damn good one—and he wasn't about to let anyone get less than his absolute best.

Jack got down on all fours, shifted back with his arms out in front of him and popped his hips up high, stretching his legs out straight. So maybe it was a little difficult to hold his head up high when it was hanging upside down between his arms, and he could possibly have picked a better position than one that had him sticking his—

Felix made a choked-off noise next to him, and Jack angled his head slightly to see what was wrong, worried that Felix had hurt his back by not doing the pose correctly. But he was still hunched on the mat watching Jack demonstrate the position, hands clenched, eyes wide and fixed unmistakably on Jack's ass where it pushed up into the air and—oh.

Oh.

Jack wanted to preen a little, but that would be unprofessional, of course. Not to mention a little tacky and vain. But if he swayed his hips just a bit more than was necessary while walking up to the front to dismiss everyone, well, he was just energized after a good session, was all.

He stood by the door, exchanging a constant stream of *Goodbye* and *See you Tuesday*, until Murray stepped close to say out of the corner of his mouth, "I may be losing my hearing, but I sure ain't blind," with another wink as he passed by. And while Jack gaped after him, trying to figure out exactly what that was supposed to mean, Felix stopped in the doorway, nervously rubbing the back of his neck.

"Sorry I'm so hopeless," he sighed.

"You are not hopeless, Felix." Jack's fingertips settled on Felix's forearm before he caught himself and pulled back. Felix was obviously not what Jack had assumed, but still. There were lines. He was a student. "You just need to relax."

"Yeah, I... struggle with that. A bit." Felix scrunched his nose up and Jack just barely resisted the urge to bop it with his index finger.

"Well, I'm sure I can find a way to loosen you up," Jack replied, then cringed at Felix's startled expression. Way to not the cross the line there. "I—I mean. You're so tense and I can help you out. Not help you out. Relieve the tension. Not like that! Oh, God. I'm shutting up now."

Jack briefly considered dropping and assuming the downward dog position again, just so he could distract Felix long enough to make a run for it, and then never show his face at the Westside YMCA again, but then Felix gave that completely disarming bashful laugh and ducked his head.

So maybe Felix had taken his offer in the spirit he'd intended. No need to panic, just a teacher reaching out to a student in need. He could steer this conversation around to more neutral waters, no problem.

"You know, just some hands-on assistance. And that still sounds like I'm propositioning you. My sincere apologies." Jack sighed and leaned his forehead against the door frame. "I had a small breakfast. Clearly I'm delirious from hunger."

" ...Right, so. I'll see you next week?"

"Uh-huh," Jack mumbled into the wood.

"And Jack?"

"Mmm?"

"I definitely wouldn't mind having you help me relieve some tension."

By the time Jack registered what he'd said and snapped his head up, Felix was walking down the hallway, leaving him with nothing but an empty room and his own overactive mind. Well, at least that mind wasn't a swirl of worry and confusion and embarrassment anymore. Instead it was settled firmly on the impure. And more specifically on the downright indecent shift and flex of Felix's ass as he walked away.

Lilah Suzanne

Chapter Four

"So was he flirting with you or not?"

Jack shrugged and took a bite of his pretzel, meandering toward the pond as joggers and bikers whizzed past them. "I don't know," he mumbled through his mouthful.

Ducking off the main walkway, they zigzagged around the bodies sprawled out in the grass to enjoy one last tease of summer before fall rolled in, gray and chilled. Some couples lay tangled together, heads resting on stomachs. Some people managed to get lost in their own worlds despite the crowd, their iPods and magazines blocking out the hum of activity all around them. Jack had hoped that a morning out in the city would be enough to distract Lydia from her hounding. No such luck.

"He said he wanted you to relieve some tension. What else could that be?" Lydia spun to face him and crossed her arms on her chest.

He'd been trying unsuccessfully all day to put off this conversation, after she'd overheard him on the phone with their boss trying to secure some studio time for a private session. She'd questioned him relentlessly and held him hostage in his own home until he admitted it was, indeed, for Felix.

"I don't know, Lydia. He's a pretty tense person! He was a boxer. He has this pent-up energy and maybe he just wants some help." Jack waved his pretzel wildly, salt flying everywhere. He sighed and shoved the rest into his mouth. It was too salty anyway.

"Pent-up energy, you say?" Lydia said, grinning and jabbing him in the ribs with her tiny, pointy elbow.

"Mmph!" Jack listed to the side, rubbing what was sure to become a bruise and trying not to choke on the rather huge bite he'd taken, and bumped right into a passing jogger. He attempted to apologize, ingrained small-town manners being hard to shake, but the mouthful of pretzel garbled his apology, and he looked up, putting on his very best face of contrition. Even if it was Lydia's fault. Meddling, spiky-boned Lydia.

"Jack?"

No. Way.

Nine million people in the entirety of New York City, and this is who he bumped into? Literally, actually bumped into. Glistening with sweat in tiny jogging shorts and a tight tank top with his earbuds dangling down his muscled chest. Jack swallowed his bite of pretzel in one giant gulp that stuck in his throat as he croaked, "Felix?" and then started to cough.

Lydia's eyes had that look. Like the time she had taken on their building super over some creaky pipes. And they'd nearly been tossed out on the street until Jack smoothed things over with a membership to a pie-of-the-month club.

Oh no. No, no, no.

"Hi, Felix! Jack was just talking about you." Felix raised his eyebrows at that, and Jack tried really hard not to die of asphyxiation right there in the middle of Central Park. "I'm Lydia Weaver. We've spoken, but haven't met properly, and that will just not do! I run youth programming at the gym. Columbia business school graduate. Philanthropist. Advocate for the little people. And Jack's roommate, best friend and closest confidante."

Lydia reached forward, grasped Felix's hand and shook it vigorously while Jack continued to gasp for air. Felix stared at her wide-eyed before recovering and smiling politely.

"So nice to officially meet you, Lydia." He looked around her to where Jack was doubled over and wheezing. "Are you okay, Jack?"

Lydia waved him off. "He'll be fine, he does that all the time." She tipped forward, still gripping Felix's hand, and pulled him closer. "He can hold his breath for ages. All that bobbing and going down."

Felix's mouth dropped open.

Coughing finally quelled, Jack heaved a breath and swiped his hand through the air to grab feebly at Lydia. Maybe if he tossed her in the pond she would *shut up*.

"Not like that! From swimming!" Lydia clarified, clutching a hand to her chest, mock-scandalized. "Jack almost went to the Olympics. Did you know that?"

"I... no. No I didn't." Felix looked over Lydia's head to where Jack was gathering himself back together and one corner of his mouth tipped up in a small smile.

"A man of many talents, huh? I'd love to watch you sometime."

Jack's stomach swooped and he cleared his throat to reply, still shaky: "I don't swim anymore." Felix tipped his head and studied Jack closely, and Jack really, really didn't want to talk about it. Not here. Not now. Not ever, preferably. So to derail the subject he quipped, "Though I do look fantastic in a Speedo."

Felix's eyes briefly dropped down Jack's body. "I bet," he murmured. Jack blushed at the attention, but held Felix's gaze steadily when his eyes flitted back up. Definitely flirting. Well, at least Jack wasn't reading too much into things. For once.

Felix lifted the hem of his shirt to wipe away the sweat beading on his brow, offering a brief glimpse of his stomach, defined abdominals damp and hollowing with each panting breath.

Jack's fingers itched to touch and he murmured without thinking, "Yes. Pretty fantastic, indeed."

Felix's head tipped to the side, mouth slowly curving into a grin.

"Well!" Lydia crowed, bringing the world crashing back down. "This is perfect!"

Jack really wished he'd thrown her into the polluted pond water when he'd had his chance.

"What is perfect, Lydia?"

"That we ran into Felix at the park here so you could tell him how there isn't any available studio space for private lessons." Lydia clapped her hands in front of her, looking entirely too pleased with herself.

He knew that look all too well. "That's right, I can't do a private lesson. Sorry, Fe—"

"At the gym!" Lydia cut in. "He can't do it at the gym, but he does them at home all the time!"

"No, I—"

"And because I am such a generous person and an accommodating, thoughtful roommate, I am more than happy to give you two time to work together. Privately. One-on-one. Relieve some tens—"

"Thank you Lydia, we get it!" God, he really needed to get her a muzzle. He gave Felix another apologetic look and said, "I think it's time for her medication—we should be going. See you in class!" as he grabbed a protesting Lydia by the arm and started to lead her away. What was this fixation on his love life lately? Was he that pathetic?

31

So most of his attempts at relationships had fizzled out before they even really began. And he'd read into a few too many polite interactions. And hooking up at a bar was so not his thing. He just wanted someone kind and romantic and funny and smart and handsome. Someone he connected with. Something that didn't seem as if he was forcing it to work. Was that so much to ask, really?

"That sounds great," Felix called. Jack let go of Lydia and spun around.

"What does?" Crap. Had he been thinking out loud again?

"The session. At your house," Felix clarified. "Do you have your phone?"

Jack fumbled in his pockets, *why did he have so many pockets*, until he finally found it tucked in the inside seam of his vest because he was wearing the jeans that accentuated his waist and legs and made him look taller—at least he had that going for him today—and handed it over. Lydia squealed and clutched at his arm, and Jack shrugged her off, silencing her with a glare.

Okay, maybe her annoying need to take charge of any situation, even if it had nothing to do with her, was occasionally useful. He'd tell her that later. Like after she stopped acting like a twelve-year-old girl meeting her favorite boy band member.

"Just text me and let me know where and when…" Felix started to tap at the screen, pursing his lips a little; then they curled into an "O" and his fingers froze over the phone. He hastily handed it back, his body already turned to start running again.

"I have to go."

Jack didn't even have a chance to respond before Felix took off across the grassy field and back onto the footpath. Bewildered, Jack watched him until he disappeared around a bend.

"What was that about?" Lydia asked.

"I have no idea, but it's starting to become a theme for us." Jack tried to shrug it off, squaring his shoulders and taking a deep breath as he went to pocket his phone. Oh no.

How could he have been so careless? On the screen was Felix's name and number. Already listed in his contacts. From when he'd found it in the computer database and entered it. Like a giant, creepy stalker.

And now he was finally starting to understand everyone's interest in fixing his love life.

Lilah Suzanne

Chapter Five

Not surprisingly, Felix didn't show up to the next class, and a small, shallow part of Jack was relieved: the part that wanted to pretend the whole incident never happened so he could just brush it aside and carry on. He couldn't, of course. Couldn't stop feeling mortified and guilty. Couldn't stop thinking about Felix and the way Felix had looked at him; so sweet and flirty, but with something more brooding and opaque behind his eyes.

Jack thought he'd found a kindred spirit in Felix, had recognized something in the set of his jaw and the hunch of his shoulders. He too was carrying the weight of the world, the way Jack had felt before he walked away from swimming and learned to breathe again.

Felix was, however, exactly where Jack had expected him to be. Jack stood off to the side wondering just how often Felix came down here to vent his frustrations and take out his anger on swaying bags of sand. He could almost see the anger, thrumming below Felix's skin and pulled tight over the straining muscles of his arms, the sharp angles of his bones, the lurch of his body as he hit the bag over and over.

It should frighten him, maybe. But he had seen Felix's tenderness, the vulnerability he kept tucked in close to his heart. It was something Jack understood, even though he had protected his own fragile heart by pushing everything and everyone away, instead of using his fists.

So no matter how angry Felix was, Jack knew he had to make things right and then back off. If Felix still wanted anything to do with him, Jack would just have to let him take the lead. And he really needed to stop being weird. Starting with removing himself from the corner where he watched Felix box, in shorts and a white tank practically see-through with sweat.

Not being creepy. Right.

Jack drew himself up to his full height, lifted his chin high and strode across the room, taking a deep breath. "I apologize for taking your phone number from our member database. I was concerned about you after you left your first day, but it was unprofessional and inappropriate and if you would like to drop my class, I understand."

Jack refilled his lungs and nodded to himself. He'd worked on perfecting that speech all weekend and was pleased to note that he'd delivered it flawlessly.

Felix paused briefly with his hands tucked close to his body, then flicked his head to the side and resumed punching. Jack clasped his own hands behind his back and watched, unsure of what to do or say. He hadn't really thought past the part where he said his piece. A bit of an oversight, he had to admit.

"So... I'll just be going, then..."

The only response was the dull thunk, thunk, thunk of Felix's gloved hands connecting with the punching bag. Jack lifted up on his toes to turn away when Felix stopped the rapid-fire movement of his fists.

"It was a total knockout."

"A what?" Jack froze in place.

"My last fight. Knockout. Second round, just flattened me." Felix gestured with his right hand, jabbing the glove through the air like a cobra striking, and then rubbed the padded end of the glove against his temple. "The concussion was so bad that I needed surgery to stop the bleeding in my brain. They told me I couldn't fight anymore. That if it happened again it would kill me."

"Felix, I had no idea. That must have been awful."

Felix shrugged and laughed humorlessly, his hands falling limp at his sides. "But you know what the worst part was? Not the pain. Not the humiliation. Not the fact that I blamed myself for screwing everything up and ruining my life." Felix turned back to the bag and hit it once, hard, but

37

he was off-center and unbalanced and stumbled forward until his shoulder came to rest against the vinyl. "The worst part was being broken and alone and realizing that no one cared. If I didn't have championship titles or sponsors or a cut of my winnings to give them, they didn't care. I was nothing to them. Nothing."

Jack stood, sad and stunned, as Felix stripped off his gloves and tucked them under one arm. All the fight seemed to have drained out of him. His eyes softened, and a tremor of a smile flickered on his lips.

"And then I was here, and the bags were all taken, so I was just wandering around lost. I saw your class and a sign-up sheet and I thought *what the hell,* you know? *Not like I have anything else going on.* And then there you were." Felix's eyes studied Jack intently. "You saw me, Jack. Me. And you cared. You don't even know me, and you care about me. And to tell you the truth that kind of scares the shit out of me."

"Oh," Jack breathed, unsure of how to respond. Felix had been through so much more than Jack could have imagined. Jack knew he had a tendency to come on too strong and that he probably cared too much. But Felix was still here. Opening up to him. And Jack still cared.

"Well, if it makes things any easier, I was less motivated by altruism and much more by the fact that you have really nice eyes."

Felix stared at him for a beat, then broke into a grin, a full one, and shook his head. "You really are something else."

Jack shrugged a shoulder. "That does seem to be the overriding theme of my life, yes."

Felix planted his free hand on a cocked hip and said, "Come here," as he held out the boxing gloves with the other. "Put these on."

Jack stepped closer and wrinkled his nose. "Are they sweaty?"

"Probably," Felix replied, slipping the first one over Jack's hand. "You have something against getting sweaty?"

"Depends on the occasion," Jack quipped, letting Felix tighten both straps with a speculative hum. "So what are we doing?"

"You're going to teach me yoga and as payment, I'll teach you to box."

"I generally prefer cash. Or a gift card to Whole Foods at the very least."

"Shhh, focus." Felix settled his hands on Jack's shoulders, positioning him directly in front of the punching bag. "Now, plant your feet, like that, yeah. And bend your knees." Felix's hands slid from Jack's shoulders and down his arms as he moved closer, speaking into Jack's ear from behind. "Keep your arms tucked in. You always want to remember to be defensive and not just go in for the attack. Keep your guard up."

Jack bent his arms in front of his face and tried bouncing on his toes, though he imagined the effect was more Tigger than Tyson. Felix chuckled, his warm breath puffing against Jack's neck and spreading heat out across his skin.

"Focus on using your shoulders and legs for strength." Felix's hands trailed back up, from shoulder to shoulder, then fleetingly touched Jack's thighs. "You have really strong shoulders. I always admired that about swimmers."

He lips brushed Jack's ear. "Always had a thing for blonds, too."

Jack shivered with the touch but narrowed his eyes and tried to focus on sending energy to his core, on breathing deeply, on trying not to think about the heat of Felix's body; the tremors left in the wake of his hands; the heady scent of him, inviting and inebriating; his voice murmuring low in Jack's ear, breath hot against the shell.

"Excellent focus. *Now*, Jack."

He hit the bag one-two, one-two, one-two, the blows reverberating through the gloves and his skin and humming in his bones.

"Good, right?"

Jack turned, his eyes finding Felix's hopeful and searching.

"Yeah," Jack replied. "That was… pretty intense."

Felix circled around him and reached to remove the gloves from Jack's tingling hands.

"That was power. Strength. The only time I ever felt safe was when I was fighting, as strange as that sounds." Felix tucked the gloves under one arm, opening and closing one dangling strap with a harsh rip of velcro.

"It makes sense," Jack shrugged. "Like you said, you have to keep your guard up."

Felix offered a half-smile. "Maybe I could try letting it down a little."

Jack's heart gave a little flutter in his chest. "Well in that case, I solemnly swear that I will not knock you out."

Felix tipped his head, eyes low, lips softly curved.

"I think it may be a little too late for that, Jack."

Lilah Suzanne

Chapter Six

The damn throw pillows had been frustrating him all morning. He'd decided to add a few more in blue velvet to highlight the subtle stitching on the larger patterned pillows behind them, but as he passed the couch again after sweeping the kitchen he sighed and removed them. Then he put two back. Then removed them again. Maybe he should move the larger ones and keep just the smaller. What was the exact number of pillows that said: Please sit, make yourself at home, and if you happen to be so comfortable that we end up making out a little, well, that is perfectly reasonable?

"Jack."

"We need different pillows. These are all wrong." Jack shook his head and gathered all of them into his arms.

"Jack."

"No. It's not the pillows, you're right." He tossed them all to the side of the couch. "It's the whole thing. It's hideous. Why do we have such a hideous couch, and how have I never noticed that?"

"I really don't think Felix cares about our pillows or our hideous couch, Jack," Lydia pointed out, slamming the refrigerator and brandishing a take-out container at him.

"Aha! So you admit it; it is hideous." Jack flopped down onto the offending couch with a frustrated huff. Great. It was uncomfortable, too. Now Felix would never want to make out.

Lydia just watched his struggle bemusedly and neatly set styrofoam containers on the counter. "Wow, you really like him."

"Shut up," Jack snapped.

"Jack and Felix sittin' in a tree, K-I-S-S-I-N-G," she sang back, swaying back and forth as she poked at her food.

Jack groaned louder, slumped forward on the uncomfortable, ugly, horrible couch and pressed his face into a cushion. "God, I hope so."

"Okay, okay." Lydia snagged one of the containers and marched briskly past the couch, clearing her throat and going into *let's get shit done* mode. "If the couch is bothering you that much, we can fix it. How about a blanket over the top? Blankets lead to cuddles. Cuddles lead to kissing. Kissing leads to—" She opened the hall closet and tossed a look back at Jack on the couch. "Whatever it is you like to do after that."

Jack jumped up. "Yes! Thank you! Uh. I think."

He crouched down in front of the closet, pushing aside plastic bins filled with books and random knickknacks, keepsakes and vases and old clothes he'd been meaning to donate. "Where's that one your mom sent for your birthday?"

"The zebra print Sherpa throw? The one you threatened to burn on sight?" She tucked her food in the crook of her elbow, stood on her toes and pulled the throw from the top shelf.

"Yeah, but it is comfortable." Jack looked up and wrinkled his nose. "Jeez, it's even uglier than I remembered. Never mind."

He shoved aside the bins, searching at the very back of the closet, where the cardboard box his parents had forced on him when they turned his childhood bedroom into a scrapbooking studio sat dusty and crumpled.

He'd almost forgotten about it. Almost.

Over two decades' worth of ribbons and plaques, trophies and certificates were in there. His first pair of goggles. Framed photos of his neighborhood swim club, his high school team, his elite college relay teammates. The ghosts of people, of places, of a person he barely remembered being.

"Do you think you're hyper-focusing on the couch because you're actually afraid of screwing things up for good with this guy?" Lydia mumbled through a mouthful of food.

"I thought you were a business major, not a psychol—God, Lydia, what are you eating? Rotting feet?" Jack covered his nose and mouth with his elbow and rose up from the floor, eyes watering.

"Oh. It's called stinky tofu, but it's delicious, I swear. Want some?" Lydia offered him a wobbling, greasy spoonful as he backed away.

"I'll pass, thanks," Jack replied, struggling to open the old painted-over window in the living room. "Ugh, it's stinking up the whole apartment." The window budged just a crack and started to creak open when the intercom buzzed.

"Oh crap, he's early!" Jack looked around the apartment in a panic at the pillows in a pile on the floor, the contents of the closet strewn all over the hall—and the smell, oh God, the smell.

"Let him up, then get rid of that. Eat it. Throw it away. Set it on fire and send it back to the sulfurous depths of hell from whence it came, I don't really care which."

Lydia made a face as she pushed the button to let Felix into the building, then dumped the carton in the trash and bagged it up. "Fine. I need to get to work early anyway. I'll just drop this off on my way out." She winked and tossed her hair over her shoulder, calling out, "Have fun!" as she strode out the door.

Jack hastily threw the pillows back onto the couch and glared at them. Nothing about that arrangement encouraged making out at all.

"Jack?" He startled and looked up to see Felix poking his head through the open door cautiously. "I saw Lydia on the way up, she said to go ahead in?"

"Yes," Jack smiled and gestured for him to come in. No need to panic, Felix was here now, time to be cool, calm and collected. "I have the mats set out by the window. Go ahead and pick one. I'll just clean this up and be right there. Sorry about the smell."

Cramming the contents of the closet back in with his foot, Jack struggled against the tide of junk resisting his efforts to close the door and grimaced when the box tipped forward and bounced the door open. It fell on its side and its contents went skidding across the floor and spread with a clatter across the hallway.

"I swear I am actually a very neat, organized person," Jack sighed as Felix started to pick up some of the paper certificates and ribbons that had fluttered out of Jack's reach. "There just isn't much closet space. Not much space period, but that's the price you pay for living in New York. What I wouldn't give for a walk-in closet." Jack rambled.

Felix had paused, arms outstretched, and he looked from a yellowing paper to Jack and back again. "Are these yours?" He picked up another one and smiled. "Second place, Little Squirts. Aww, look at the happy little whale cartoon, that's adorable."

Felix gathered up the papers and ribbons—all of Jack's awards and participatory certificates that his parents had saved from the time he was barely more than an infant until he quit—while Jack squirmed with anxiety.

"Oh. Um," Jack took it all from Felix's hands and shoved it back in the box. "My parents are little overly sentimental. My mom saved all my baby teeth, too." He widened his eyes and whispered, "It's all very disturbing."

Felix laughed, a full, throaty thing, and Jack felt warm from head to toe. He was so lost in smiling back that he missed Felix reaching into the box. "Oh, wow." Jack looked down, his churning stomach sinking. "So, we should get started," he said, taking the gold plaque out of Felix's hands and putting everything back into the dark corner of the closet where it belonged.

"Lydia wasn't exaggerating. You were headed to the Olympics."

"It was just a qualifier." Jack stood and brushed his hands on his pants.

"An Olympic qualifier that you placed first in. And all those blue ribbons and trophies. You were obviously really good, Jack."

"*Were*," Jack said tightly. "Almost my entire life was swimming, as soon as I could toddle into the shallow end, and for what? Guess how many employers care about my blue ribbons or my trophies? There was no point to any of it."

Felix frowned, eyebrows drawn, eyes serious and searching Jack's face. "Didn't you love it, though? Wasn't that the point?"

Jack's throat felt tight and his heart thumped unevenly in his chest. Maybe he did love it, once upon a time. But not anymore. "It doesn't matter now," he answered with a sad smile. "Shall we?"

Jack walked to his mat and eased himself down, bending his legs until his thighs spread apart and the soles of his feet touched. "Just a simple butterfly pose to start and some deep breathing."

"It's not too late, you know. You're young still. Besides, plenty of athletes compete into their forties. Or even later." Felix flopped down across from him and Jack flicked his gaze away.

"Mmm. Let's try a lotus pose now."

"Or just start training again and do local meets. Don't even stress about higher-level competition. "

Jack sighed and tried not to lose control of his breathing. "You aren't paying attention. Lotus."

"Or just compete with yourself! Maybe you can beat your old times."

"Felix."

"Jack."

Jack looked away from his focal point on the wall to where Felix's knees were bent and almost touching his own, fingers curved over them. His eyebrows were raised expectantly.

"Look, for a long time I did love it. Nothing made me happier than getting in the water and just—" Jack looked out the window, over the buildings and into the blue sky beyond. "Just flying, you know? But it started to be too much, and I didn't love it. I dreaded every second and I couldn't figure out why I kept making myself miserable. Then one day

I—I had enough. So I stopped." Jack shrugged. "It's fine."

Felix's fingers fanned out to brush against Jack's. "I'm sorry. I didn't mean to push. You were obviously very good, and I hate to see anyone give up on a dream."

Jack tentatively reached his own fingers out to tangle with Felix's. "I know. But I'm good at this, too. Sometimes dreams change."

"Sometimes they're snatched away from you." Felix's hands flexed, curling Jack's tightly in his grasp. "If you still have the option, Jack, you shouldn't just give up."

"I've moved on, okay," Jack snapped, pulling his hands away and shifting into a kneeling position. "Now lunge."

Breathing deeply, Jack calmed with each slow exhalation and the familiar burn and ache of his muscles as he stretched and pushed them to the limit. Felix was being intrusive, but it wasn't as if he'd said anything that Jack hadn't thought already, late at night, after another day of just getting by, just existing.

He often relived the day when he'd felt suffocated by everyone else's expectations, everyone else's dreams for him, when he was unsure of what he even wanted anymore, and how it all came to a head in the worst way and Jack walked away with humiliation and shame weighing him down.

How a yoga class with Lydia months later was the first time he felt as if he could breathe again. How he walked out of the class feeling lighter. How, that night, he fell asleep without thinking about swimming at all. And so he'd stayed there, because he was terrified of what would be waiting for him when he gave those thoughts a chance to come back.

Now, his frustration building, shoulders pulling too tight, lungs filling and emptying shallowly, frantically, Jack went automatically into a more intense workout; he needed something more challenging to channel his energy. He squatted, back curved and limbs tucked in, and then lifted up so he was supported completely by his arms, his legs pulled up tight, his body suspended and curved like an apostrophe. Breathe. In. Out.

"Ah!" A thud broke his concentration, then a muffled huff of laughter, and Jack lowered himself next to where Felix was splayed on his stomach, his face pressed into the floor. "I think that may be too advanced for me," Felix said, turning over onto his back with a grin.

"Right. Sorry about that," Jack looked away, studying the dust motes dancing and twirling in the beam of light from the open window. "Maybe I haven't moved on completely."

"Yeah, I guess I know how that feels," Felix replied, lifting his hand to brush a lock of hair gilded by the sun away from Jack's forehead. Jack leaned

51

into the touch and swallowed, his Zen breathing now catching quickly.

Felix smiled and laughed. "You should have warned me about yoga injuries. I think I'm mortally wounded," he said, still sprawled on the floor, rubbing his nose with the heel of his hand.

Jack rolled his eyes. "Oh right, I can see how much you're suffering."

"I really am." Felix reached his arms up, tucked them behind his head and darted his tongue out to wet his lips.

"Hmm," Jack hesitated, eyes dropping from Felix's mouth to his low-lidded eyes and back again. Then quickly leaned down to drop a kiss on the tip of Felix's nose. "Better?"

"Not quite." Felix's hand came up again to cup Jack's jaw and gently pulled him down for a kiss, his lips warm and soft and pliant, then pulled away, eyes searching Jack's with that familiar look of hope and hesitance, as if he was afraid of his own feelings, his own desires.

Jack surged down to press their mouths together, slipping his hand into Felix's short hair to better angle the kiss. Felix breathed in harshly through his nose. His lips parted, and Jack took the opportunity to nip at them gently.

Felix let out a quiet whimper, and Jack licked into his mouth, Felix twitching and panting out breaths beneath the solid press of Jack's body, clutching at Jack's back and letting him take control. Jack shifted onto his elbows so he could hold Felix's head in both hands. The pad of his thumb found the scar on Felix's temple and traced the line of it all the way up, then back down, saying with his lips and his tongue and his breath and his touch: *It's okay to want this. I promise I won't hurt you.*

Jack slotted his leg between Felix's, up to where he found Felix growing hard already, and felt dizzy with it all: Felix beneath him. Felix's whimpered moans and rocking hips. Felix taking and responding, so perfectly. Jack wanted. Wanted like he hadn't in… ever. He'd never felt this kind of connection with anyone; white-hot desire spread like wildfire through his veins, and all he could think was more, more, more.

"Jack," Felix groaned.

"Bedroom," Jack choked out. "We can. I want to." But Felix stopped him with a hand on Jack's arm, a look of regret in his eyes.

"No," he replied.

Lilah Suzanne

Chapter Seven

Jack scrambled back immediately, icy cold shame stamping out the flames of desire. He'd read the situation wrong. Once again, he was looking so hard for love that he'd forced a relationship where there wasn't one. Made the entire thing up in his head. What if Felix wasn't even interested in him like that?

But they had been flirting, he was sure of it. For weeks now.

And Felix had kissed him.

"No?" Jack repeated, willing his voice to come out confident, challenging. Not shaky. Not hurt.

Felix sat up and scrubbed his fingers through his hair. "God, I'm screwing this up already." He crooked his legs and took Jack's hand, folded it between his own. "Look, I've done the hooking up thing, and I don't want—not that I don't want to! I do, you are so—I mean, look at you… "

Jack frowned and looked down at himself: soft cotton shirt, yoga pants, bare feet. Hardly anything to get excited about. "If you think this is thrilling, you should see me on laundry day. I'm talking holey jeans, stained shirts. It'll knock your socks off."

Felix flashed a grin and looked down at their joined hands. "I really like you, Jack. A lot. And I want to do this right."

Jack had been mostly kidding about the persuasive power of Felix's eyes, but when he looked up the sunlight was catching Felix's face, his irises like cracked earth, rich and solemn and deep. But more than that, there was just so much in the way he looked at Jack. Jack didn't understand why or what he'd done to cause it. But he badly wanted to be whatever it was that Felix saw.

" ...Do you? Is that okay?"

Jack realized with a start that Felix had been talking to him. Asking him something, more specifically. His cheeks flushed red at the realization that he had actually gotten lost in Felix's eyes.

He should say yes. Yes was a safe answer. Unless Felix had just proposed that they go to an orgy. That didn't sound like Felix but he should say no, just in case.

"Um?" Jack finally said. He squeezed his eyes closed immediately after the sound had left his mouth.

But Felix laughed softly. "Okay, I'll ask again. Will you go out with me, Jack?"

"Like a date?" Jack peeked one eye open.

"Yes, exactly like a date," Felix replied warmly.

They made plans for Saturday. Felix insisted on picking Jack up and making the dinner reservations, claiming it was only fair, as he'd done the asking. Throughout the rest of the session, it was teasing touches and silly grins and Jack's heart felt light and free.

When Felix finally left, hours after he'd arrived, Jack couldn't resist pressing one last parting kiss to Felix's smiling mouth before he ducked out the door.

Which, of course, was when Lydia came back, raising a hand to her head in a dramatic pantomime of a swoon behind Felix's back. Jack rolled his eyes and closed the door behind her and tasked himself with eradicating the last of the lingering, pungent smell of Death By Tofu from the apartment with a bottle of Febreze. Then he chased a squealing Lydia around with it, too. Just to be thorough.

He felt as though he was floating the entire week, running through his classes and errands and morning yoga routine on automatic, turning giddy and breathless whenever Felix sent him a sweet text.

Do you have any allergies? (No.)
Is a dozen roses overkill? (Probably.)
Japanese food? (Yes. Very much yes.)
and
I can't stop thinking about you, is that weird?
(No.)

He'd found himself at the Park Slope Flea Market, browsing the vendors' stalls and sipping a green juice to make up for the churro he'd caved on earlier. Lydia had fallen behind to argue with a vendor over the price of a beaded necklace, and Jack meandered on, a pleasant, cool breeze ruffling his hair, a steel drum clanging merrily in the distance, the crowd a buzz of cheerful activity.

He stopped at a table loaded with satin and silk in all manner of forms: scarves, head wraps, ties and vests and even shirts with shiny pearl buttons. He picked up a tie the light green of an ocean shallow and ran it softly through his hand. It shimmered like a rolling wave. Perfect.

Lydia went out for the evening, and Jack was left with plenty of time to fix his hair, then wash it out and fix it again, trying for casually mussed spikes that didn't look as if they had taken him an hour to perfect.

He triple-checked the fit of his pants, twisting in the full-length mirror to make sure they still made his ass look as great as he remembered, scrutinized his pores and brushed his teeth. Again. He was just starting to get irritated with the couch and throw pillows once more when the buzzer went off.

Jack was extremely grateful that Lydia had gone out earlier, because this time he was most definitely swooning.

"Felix," Jack breathed out in a whoosh. Felix shifted on the spot in fitted slacks, a button-down pulled tight around his biceps and a vest that just made his broad chest look broader. His hair was neatly combed and his face freshly shaved and spots of color flushed his cheeks.

He looked stunning.

"Hi." Felix pulled an arm from behind his back and thrust forward a bouquet of orange tulips with whorls of yellow feathering across the petals. "Um, these are for you."

Jack had an overwhelming moment of wanting to shout, "Forget the date," grab Felix by his waist and hold him captive in the bedroom. But Felix had gotten them reservations at one of the hottest sushi places in Manhattan and had been excitedly texting Jack their menu for the past few days; and judging from the way he bounced from foot to foot and grinned, he seemed very pleased with himself for setting up this whole thing.

So instead, Jack took the flowers and grinned back and thanked him, ushering him inside with a kiss to his warm cheek. A whiff of shaving cream and soap and a woodsy cologne made Jack's pulse flutter and skip, and he could feel the heat of Felix's gaze as he stretched to retrieve a vase from the high cabinet over the fridge.

"You look amazing," Felix said, sidling up to Jack as he snipped the flower stems and settled them into the water. "I like your tie. Matches your eyes."

"Thank you," Jack smiled, positioning the vase so it could soak up the sunlight first thing in the morning. "You clean up rather nicely, I must say."

59

Felix lifted his chin to tug at his collar, sending a vision flashing through Jack's mind of his fingers replacing Felix's and deftly unbuttoning it, then leaning in to brush his lips and tongue along Felix's bobbing Adam's apple. Jack shook off the vision and cinched his tie a little tighter.

"It's been a while since I've had an occasion to get dressed up. I guess the whole cut-off sweats and ratty T-shirt combo wasn't doing much for me, huh?" Felix asked.

Jack gave in to the urge and brushed his fingers along Felix's collar, tugging it down to straighten it, even though it didn't need it. Felix looked perfect. But then, he always did.

Felix's hands grasped at nothing in the air, as if he was looking for something else to grab onto. Something other than Jack. He gasped a breath and swallowed and Jack watched his throat move, transfixed. "I wouldn't say that."

Felix gave in and jerked forward to clasp his fingers tightly around Jack's shoulders, pulling him closer and tipping forward as he captured Jack's lips in his own. Jack spread his hands out over either side of Felix's jaw, feeling the shift and flex of it as they worked their mouths together. He shuddered out a breath after they pulled away.

"I changed my mind," Felix said, chasing after Jack's mouth and stealing another kiss. "I want to. I really, really want to."

60

Jack thumbed along the line of his jaw, sliding their lips together again, then again, wanting nothing more than to stay there, just slip under and drown himself in Felix's touch and his lips and his strength. Everything about Felix felt right. Felix was right.

But Jack forced himself to step back. Going out, getting to know each other better—that was right, too. "If you think you're getting out of spending your life savings on buying me all the sushi I can eat, you are sorely mistaken." He turned and hooked his elbow out.

"Shall we?"

Felix grinned and linked their arms together. "We shall."

The date was wonderful. Easy, comfortable, familiar. Jack found himself enamored of the way Felix's nose crinkled when they joked together, the solid weight of his palm over Jack's when they talked about the trials of their pasts, the way he rested his temple on his knuckles and looked away whenever the conversation got too serious.

Jack leaned back against the end of the bar at the front of the restaurant as Felix settled the bill and watched the smooth, easy flow of his body as he stood and slid his wallet into his pocket, tracked him as he walked across the dim room, gliding gracefully around tables and patrons, something so quietly powerful in the way he moved. Then Felix spotted him from the other end of the bar and a radiant grin spread, slow and sure, across his face.

"Can I buy you drink?"

Jack's attention shifted, dragged reluctantly away from Felix pushing through the crowd to join him at the bar, and he spared a brief glance at the man who had leaned much too far into Jack's personal space. The man was bleary-eyed and clumsy, and his bloodshot gaze roved over Jack's body.

Jack stiffened and angled away from him. "No, thank you."

His eyes sought out Felix again, his nerves pulsing in warning at the unwanted attention and still more insistently when he was unable to spot Felix among the laughter and drinking and flirting and inane conversation surrounding him.

"Okay then, how about we just go right to the part where you come home with me?"

That Jack didn't even bother to acknowledge. Instead, he stood up from the bar, lengthening his spine and angling his shoulders and elbows and hips so he looked bigger, imposing. There was no chance in hell, even if he hadn't been on a date.

"I'm here with someone," Jack said shortly. Felix popped out of the crowd looking flustered, his clothes a little disheveled, as if he'd had to fight his way through. "And we were just leaving."

The guy smelled like alcohol and stale sweat. He lumbered unsteadily to grasp at Jack's elbow as he started to walk off, misjudged the distance and pressed his clammy chest along Jack's arm.

All of Jack's defenses snapped in at once: his body went rigid, his lip curled in disgust and he readied himself to send the guy away with a shove and a cutting remark. But Felix got there first.

Jack's arm was released so quickly he stumbled forward, and his drunken would-be suitor was suddenly thrown against the bar and scrambled, disoriented, for equilibrium as glasses and bottles scattered. Jack heard the unpleasant clang of glass on glass, sloshing fluids and the gasps and murmurs of people immediately nearby.

The man put his hands up defensively and slunk along the bar as Felix rounded on him, his eyes gone narrow and dark, his jaw clenched, that current of hot fury emanating from every inch of him: dangerous. Blinding. Desperate.

"Hey," Jack said, stepping in front of Felix, trying to catch his fixed gaze, to break him free. "Felix." His fingertips grazed Felix's arm and Felix flinched away, wild-eyed, then spun to face him, both arms coming up reflexively into fists, ready to fight.

Forgotten, the guy lurched away into the watching crowd, and for a moment Jack worried that Felix was unreachable or angry with him. That he thought Jack had actually been interested in someone else. The air hung heavy between them as Jack waited. As the crowd around them waited.

"Jack." Anger cracked into heartbreak, and something shattered behind Felix's eyes as his posture dropped, spent. "I'm so sorry, I—"

Jack swooped in, close but not close enough—not in public, not with an audience. "Hey, hey, shhh. It's okay. Outside. It's okay. Just breathe."

The barest touch of their arms connected them physically until they got outside into the warm, humid night air of New York in the summer and walked down the street. They turned a corner into an alleyway where trash spilled from cans and crates were stacked high amid sticky puddles.

Then Felix was in his arms, tight and trembling, breathing out in a mantra against Jack's neck.

" ...Sorry, so sorry. I wasn't. I would never hurt you, I wasn't..."

And Jack shushed him, smoothed his twisted shirt and rubbed circles across his back. "I know. I know you wouldn't. He was just some drunk idiot. He's not worth it."

Jack slid a hand down Felix's arm, tangling their fingers together and pressing them between their bodies, his stomach rising and falling steadily and slowly against Felix's own panted breaths.

"I saw him touch you and I just snapped." A heaving sigh, a tremor flashed quickly across his shoulders. "I still have all this anger and I don't know what to do with it anymore and I'm terrified, Jack." He stepped back, still holding tightly to Jack's hand, and even in the dark Jack was brought up short by the depths of Felix's eyes. "It just felt like—like I finally found you and I was losing you already."

Jack was struck dumb by Felix's declaration: what it meant, what Felix needed from him. His instinct was to retreat, to crack a joke, to wave a hand around airily and declare that Felix had only found him because Jack's overinflated nurturing instinct refused to take no for an answer. Instead he said nothing. Because he needed Felix too. Hadn't he known that from the start?

His eyes roved over Felix's shadowed form, still drawn up tense and guarded, head turned away to the light pooling yellow from a street lamp. Then he moved in to press a hard kiss to Felix's lips and a whimper of surprise startled from Felix's throat.

"Me too. I don't want to lose you either."

Felix kissed back, mouth closed but seeking, wanting. "If you still want to, I live close by. Is that—"

"Yes," Jack exhaled, pressing back, giving, taking. "Yes."

Lilah Suzanne

Chapter Eight

"Oh, it's very... cozy," Jack decided, stepping past Felix and into his studio apartment after a short but fairly tense cab ride. The place was small. Really, really small. The furniture and decorations were minimalist and warm, organized but lived-in. Jack noted a crocheted blanket hung over the back of a tan leather couch, scuffed wood floors and piles of books and magazines on almost every flat surface. But it was also clean, Jack thought, as he nosed around in the main room. The two windows' hunter green shades were pulled closed and the kitchen along the back wall was narrow but fully equipped. A bathroom was tucked in the corner, and Jack saw a ladder leading to—

"Ooh, a loft bed," Jack said, tipping his head up to look over the low ceiling above the kitchen. The edge of a mattress was just visible. "Totally urban-chic."

Felix gathered a collection of books into his arms and dropped them on a high shelf, giving Jack a wan smile. "That is a very diplomatic way of saying that I literally sleep in a hole in the wall," he said.

Jack waved a dismissive hand. "No, it's very in. Very European. I read an article about it at the dentist." He stepped over to the ladder. "Can I?"

Felix raised his eyebrows, nodded. "Go for it."

Jack scaled the ladder and climbed onto the bed, only realizing how forward he was being after he'd settled into the muted light of the little alcove in the ceiling. "Wow, I just invited myself into your bed."

Felix smiled and crawled across the bed. He sat next to Jack and kicked his shoes off carelessly. They clunked onto the floor below, and Felix gestured to Jack's boots. "Yeah, I wish I'd known sooner what a great pick-up line 'Would you like to see my sleeping cubby?' would be. Could have saved myself a lot of trouble."

Jack slipped one boot off and gently set it aside, raising his eyebrows at Felix, who winked in response. Jack hummed, got the other boot off and crossed his legs under him in lotus pose to face Felix. "So I take it you're feeling better, then?"

Felix tensed and turned away. "Can we just forget that happened?"

"Nope."

"Jack."

"Felix."

Felix sighed, bent his knees and wrapped both arms around his legs like a cage. "It was stupid and I shouldn't have—you can obviously take care of yourself, and I'm not just some meathead who gets into bar brawls, I'm not."

"So why did you snap, then?" Jack tentatively leaned over to rub a hand along Felix's back: hard knots of muscle over hollow, curving bones. Felix dropped his head to his arms, melted into the touch as if he was carved from ice and Jack was the hot lick of flames.

"It just brought up some old stuff that I'd rather not deal with, okay?"

"Okay," Jack passed his hand up and down the hunch of Felix's back, feeling the muscles loosen and clench again under his palm. "Can we try something?"

Felix lifted his head, a mischievous grin playing on his lips.

"Not like that," Jack clarified. Felix stuck his lip out in a pout that was probably meant to be sexy. It sort of was. "Come on," Jack laughed, moving to a kneeling position. His spiked-up hair just brushed the low ceiling. "Lie back and take your shirt off, it's too restrictive—what?"

Felix tugged at the top buttons, his warm skin and a dusting of dark hair revealed in torturous increments. "I'm getting a lot of mixed messages here, Jack." He quickly finished unbuttoning, shrugged off his shirt and scooted back against the pillows.

Jack completely forgot the point of the whole exercise at the sight of Felix's bare chest and stomach, his tawny skin over curving lines of muscle and bone, the prominent veins meandering up his arms and shoulders and a thick trail of dark hair making an enticing path that led beneath the waistband of his pants. "God, you're gorgeous," Jack whispered, realizing too late that he'd said it aloud.

Felix smiled. "So was this the whole plan? Because I think I should get a turn to ogle you. It's only fair."

Jack shook himself and batted at Felix's bent knee as he scooted closer. "No, I was going somewhere with this. We're going to try some relaxation poses. I think they could really help you."

Felix sighed dramatically. "That doesn't sound nearly as fun as what I had in mind."

"Give it a chance." Jack took a deep, cleansing breath and forced himself to transition into something resembling professionalism, his voice low and soothing. "I want you to focus on your diaphragm; fill your lungs clear down into your abdomen, then let the air out slowly. Lie in corpse pose."

Felix shifted to lie completely flat on his back, hand curled on his stomach. "You'd think they could come up with a less morbid name," he grumped, eyes screwed shut.

Jack clicked his tongue. "You have a better one in mind?"

"Mmm...sunbathing pose? Chillaxing position?" Jack coughed a laugh. Felix grinned, eyes shut tight. "Lying-half-naked-in-my-bed-with-a-really-hot-guy pose?"

"Kind of wordy, don't you think?" Jack took both of Felix's hands and stretched his arms out along either side of his body.

"Well, you'd have to use an acronym, obviously."

"Right, of course." Jack feathered his fingertips along the insides of Felix's arms, over the landscape of veins and bones and shifting tendons, across the knotted curve of his shoulders and across his chest. "I want you to breathe in slowly, as if you're filling up your diaphragm, then your lungs."

Felix did as Jack instructed. His face relaxed, his chest expanded and his stomach heaved, and Jack rested his hand there, watching the slow rise up, up, then down until Felix's belly hollowed concave once more.

"Good. Keep going, and with your next breaths imagine a cleansing energy flowing through you, gathering up the hurt and the anger, and when you breathe out, you'll release it from your body. Just let it go." Felix lifted an eyebrow and looked at Jack through slitted eyes. "Yes, I know how ridiculous that sounds, just do it."

Felix closed his eyes again and cycled through several deep breaths, the stilled air around them expanding as Felix released lungful after lungful, tension and energy swirling almost tangibly on the bed and between their bodies. Jack moved his hand to trace the curved outline of Felix's lips, the delicate membranes of his eyelids, his lush eyelashes and the scar on his temple, raised and shining and pink.

"I used to get beaten up. In school." Felix breathed in, in. Out. "Because I was too skinny. I had braces. Didn't wear the right clothes." In, in, out. "Because I was gay.

"Everyone talked about doing something. Threatening them with suspensions, which just made things worse. Maybe having me change classes or even sending me to private school." In. Out. "Nothing ever happened, though." Jack slipped his hand down again, over the steady thumping of Felix's heart, and pressed it flat just to feel the pulse against his palm.

"If I let it go, then that means I have to forgive them. Not just the people who hurt me, but the ones who didn't care enough to actually do anything about it." Felix's eyes opened and darkened, his heart picking up speed. "They don't deserve my forgiveness."

Jack fanned his fingers over Felix's sternum and pressed the tips of his fingers to the thump of Felix's heart, his chest filling with shallow breaths. "Turn over," Jack instructed.

Felix searched Jack's face, hesitating, but complied and rolled onto his stomach with Jack hunched over him. "Hands under your shoulders, elbows back. Now push your chest up and leave your hips and legs pressed down. This is cobra pose." Jack put one hand on Felix's back and one hand on his chest and pushed against his curved spine. "This will open your lungs and your heart. Let the energy flow out with every breath. Just be here, in this moment."

Jack breathed along with Felix to guide him, close to his ear, and felt his chest widen and expand under his hands, his back still knotted with pent-up tension.

"Do you?"

Felix's muscles trembled slightly with the effort of staying raised off the bed. "Do I what?"

"Do you deserve your forgiveness?" Felix's posture faltered and Jack pushed back against him to keep him steady.

Felix's head flopped down and he turned to look sadly at Jack. "I don't know," he said finally.

Jack traced down from Felix's neck to the dip of his back, tripping along the hills and valleys of vertebrae. "Forgiveness is a gift we give ourselves, Felix."

Felix's chest dropped to the bed suddenly and he flipped over, shaking his head against the pillow. "You are a very wise man, you know that?"

Jack shrugged, hooking a finger through a belt loop on Felix's pants. "Actually, I stole that quote from Suzanne Somers."

The melancholy look on Felix's face slipped away and his nose wrinkled with a wry grin.

"Suzanne Somers, really?"

"Hey, judge all you want, but that Thighmaster thing was genius. Truly one of the most under-appreciated minds of our time."

Felix smiled and brought one hand up to cup Jack's jaw. "I'm going to try."

"The Thighmaster?"

"No, silly. That whole forgiveness thing. I don't want my past to define me anymore. I don't want to keep everyone out. I don't want to be afraid."

This time it didn't feel urgent or overwhelming, but tender. The slip of tongues and slide of lips. Jack's hands, deft and sure, unbuttoning and parting his own shirt. Jack kissing a path from Felix's mouth to the hinge of his jaw, nuzzling and gliding down the slope of his neck, sucking across his chest, biting down on newly exposed hips and the sharp cut of muscles below.

Jack worked Felix's pants off, and his belt buckle jangled as Jack tossed the pants and the rest of his own clothes into the corner. He moved back up from the corner of the bed and brushed his mouth along the straining thickness of Felix's cock through his briefs, breath puffing out hot at the tip. A quiet groan rumbled from Felix's chest as his hands came down to grip Jack's hair and scrape along his scalp. "Jack."

"Let me in," Jack whispered.

Felix released him, arms going slack on the bed once more, and swallowed. "Okay."

His hands on Felix's hips, Jack marveled at how strong Felix was. Not just physically, though there was no denying the power in his body, but mentally as well. He had the fortitude to take punch after punch to the chin, to the chest, and get back on his feet still swinging time and time again.

Yet in Jack's embrace he felt so fragile, trusting Jack to open him up with care and gentleness. Trusting him with the body that had taken so much and kept right on going, with the gentle heart that had been shattered carelessly by those who were supposed to love Felix the most.

Head resting on the trembling muscles of Felix's belly, Jack hoped Felix understood just how badly he wanted to live up to that trust. And just how much Jack needed someone who thought him capable of something so important.

If you give me your heart, I promise I'll keep it safe.

Jack eased off Felix's briefs, pushed his knees up and spread them as Felix stretched out a hand to fumble in a basket tucked between the mattress and the wall. He handed a bottle and a condom to Jack, his eyes dark but trusting, body relaxed. No holding back. No guard up.

"Don't forget to breathe," Jack instructed, dipping his head down to tongue Felix's balls and the base of his shaft, softly teasing, coaxing him open. He slipped one slicked-up finger into the tight clench below, and Felix sighed, lips parted, whimpering and twitching his hips when Jack added two and then three fingers, twisting and stretching.

"I'm ready," Felix said, voice thready and rough.

Jack rose up, pushed back against Felix's thighs and moved higher to kiss Felix's lax mouth, felt him accepting, surrendering, opening to Jack as he pressed in, in.

Felix's arms came up to hold Jack's shoulders snugly and his legs twined around Jack's back, pressing them together mouth to mouth, chest to chest, heart to pounding heart as Jack's hips canted and thrusted.

Jack fucked him rhythmically, calculatedly: Stroke. Stroke. Stroke. He went at the pace of a lap swim, with the measured breathing of a yoga pose. But Felix's breaths hitched and he gasped, short bursts of *ahs* and *ohs*, his muscles straining, his fingers grasping, his mouth everywhere, eager and messy. So Jack's hips faltered in their pace as his body took over and careened chaotically toward pleasure. Hard, pounding slaps of flesh on flesh, then long, smooth strokes—it was wild, off-kilter; grabbing and moaning and biting and everything so desperate and intense, like no sex Jack had ever had.

This was no way to win a race, no way to calmly hold a pose: hold and hold and release. With Felix, Jack had no composure; no tactic to deal with the dark burn of his eyes or the hot pull of his body or just how much he meant with every single press of his lips.

Felix was overwhelming in all the best ways; a dam had broken inside Jack, in that place where he held back the stormy seas of all the difficult things he tried not to feel: the pain, yes. But the joy. The joy, too.

Jack shifted forward on his elbows to hold Felix tightly under his shoulders, the change in angle making Felix's back go rigid. He flung his head to the side, a long, low whine streaming from his throat.

"You can let go," Jack murmured, kissing Felix's clenched mouth, his cheeks, his nose, his tightly shut eyes. The scar. Felix's hips bucked up, his cock sliding and pressing into Jack's belly, his muscles balled up impossibly tight. To Felix—and to himself—Jack said, exhaling, "Let go."

Felix came with a soundless cry, arms stretched out like a bird in flight, legs dropping wide, head thrown back, neck exposed. Jack pushed up onto his hands, taking in the spread of Felix's body, so vulnerable, stripped and relaxed. Free. And Jack let it wash over him, take him away, let himself have what he given up hope of having: something *real*, risks be damned. Let himself move and move and fly. Let himself have joy.

Lilah Suzanne

Chapter Nine

The sound of a jackhammer startled Jack from a deep sleep, and the wisps of a very pleasant dream scattered as he blinked his eyes open. Sunlight streamed in from the windows on the wall opposite, and next to him Felix's strong profile was haloed in light, along with the dark stubble on his chin and cheeks and his gently parted lips. He had one arm curled behind his head. He was so peaceful, so beautiful; Jack watched him sleep and realized that a part of Felix had already slotted in next to his heart and made itself at home.

Outside, the sounds of traffic and people shouting and the constant destruction and reconstruction of the city tumbled chaotically as always; Felix snuffled and snored; and somewhere there was a ceaseless knocking. Jack felt as if he'd had the best night's sleep of his life.

He rubbed his eyes and stretched in an attempt to rouse his body and mind, and his hand collided with Felix's arm. Jack turned on his pillow, and his nose met the gentle-skinned pulse behind Felix's ear. He breathed him in, a flush of warmth flooding his body as he reached a hand out to brush over the scrub of Felix's hair. Felix grunted and shifted, the covers slipping lower on his naked waist, and Jack pulsed hot with wanting him so badly.

But despite his libido's very insistent desires, he peeled back the covers and scooted over to the ladder, shimmying on his underwear before climbing down into the bright light of the living room. Felix looked so peaceful that Jack felt rude for wanting to wake him just because he had woken up already wound tight with desire. Of course, doing his morning yoga in someone else's house in nothing but his underwear was probably not the height of etiquette. Miss Manners would be appalled.

He was just getting into the zone, body bowing and shifting and flowing through the steps of a sun salutation to greet the day, arms raised in exaltation to the ceiling, body stretching long and high then bending down, down with a smooth exhalation, when he felt warm hands tug gently on his hips and heard Felix's voice, low and rough from sleep.

"I could get used to waking up to this."

Jack laughed, a little embarrassed at being caught bent in half at the waist and sporting nothing but a pair of briefs. He'd really thought that Felix was out for the count and that he'd have time to run through a quick routine. But then Felix pressed his hips in, his hard, bare cock rubbing insistently along Jack's ass, and embarrassment quickly became the least of Jack's concerns.

Instead he unfolded himself and stood, stretching his hands back up high above his head, as Felix plastered his naked body, as hot and bright as the morning sun, against Jack's back. Felix's arms snaked around to hold tight to Jack's waist and chest, and Jack's breath quivered on a long exhalation. He gave in to his urge to nuzzle Felix's cheek with his own lightly stubbled one.

"Well, good morning," Jack teased, his own voice dropping to deep and graveled.

Felix's hand moved slowly down past Jack's turned-in bellybutton and the gentle slope of muscle below, and then scratched through the hair underneath and into his briefs to stroke his hardening cock, the other arm clasping him more tightly around the ribs. "Mmm, it really is."

Jack felt as if he was being wrapped up in Felix, whose body canted behind him solid and strong. He closed his eyes and let the sensations take over, let his mind drift and float, let his body react and mold into Felix's. His arms dropped behind their tucked-together heads to grip Felix tight as he leaned down and in to mouth, hot and wet, at Jack's neck and biceps and shoulders.

Jack shoved his underwear down to his knees and thrust up into Felix's fist and then back, spread and then tightened his thighs so Felix's cock could slot between them and press snugly under the bottom curve of his ass. Felix drove his hips in and out, the pulsing heat of his cock thrusting in under Jack's balls, slick against the base of Jack's cock, Felix's hand tight and perfect, working him over. They both moaned long and low and softly, a quiet mantra, a chant, an *om*, and came like that, together, twined around each other in a pool of sunlight as the chaos of the city carried on below.

The tiny corner bathroom was barely big enough to fit a pedestal sink of cracked porcelain, a toilet with a shelf above it and a shower in the narrow space next to that. Felix adjusted the water while Jack stood with his hip digging into the sink. His elbow banged the door when he swung it closed.

Felix hopped under the spray, beckoned Jack, then promptly slid the frosted glass, gold-handled shower door shut and yanked Jack's body to his with a firm grip on his ass.

"Handsy," Jack chided, adjusting the water to spray on his chest and shoulders instead of his face.

"It's a very confined space. I don't have anywhere else to put them," Felix replied, squeezing hard to make his point.

Jack grabbed the soap, blue and thin and slippery, rubbed Felix's chest in foaming circles and hummed, "I could think of few places you can put them."

They made out lazily until the water ran cold and then put on clothes, still damp and shivering and grinning and grinning.

Felix handed Jack sweats just a tad too short and tight across his broader shoulders and longer torso. Felix's eyes roved hungrily over him and then he ducked back into the kitchen and whipped up some truly amazing pancakes—an old family recipe, or so he claimed, but refused to give Jack the details. So he was a bit suspicious.

"If it's Betty Crocker, I promise not to judge."

"Please," Felix scoffed, flipping the last batch onto a plate. "But if you're jealous of my cooking skills, I completely understand."

Jack swallowed his bite of pancake and lifted an eyebrow. "What are you doing tomorrow night?"

"I didn't have any plans, why?" Felix set the plate down on the table, jutting out a hip. His sweatpants rode low, and he was shirtless and barefoot. To entice Jack, no doubt, and it was definitely working. And two could play that game.

"Because," Jack drawled, popping the last bite into his mouth and chewing slowly, "you're going to come over…" He swallowed deliberately and licked his lips, pleased to see Felix's eyelids slip low, a dark flush on his cheeks. "…And I am going to cook you a meal so delicious. So decadent. That it will make you weep."

Jack winked and, feeling confident, gave Felix a teasing smack on the ass as he walked to the sink to drop his plate in. Felix jumped in surprise, a grin spreading slowly on his face, and crowded Jack up against the sink, pulling him in for a syrupy kiss.

Jack was already mentally cataloguing all of his favorite gourmet recipes, trying to remember if he had any saffron left for a bouillabaisse or if it was still too early in the fall for soup; or maybe he should make that duck breast with risotto he attempted a few months ago.

Back when he had suddenly lost swimming as a focus for his energies and was no longer eating anything and everything for the thousands of calories he needed to consume and burn off during hours in the pool, he had turned to cooking to fill the extra hours. Well, engaging in Food Network marathons and feeling sorry for himself at first, then cooking. And he finally had someone to please with his skills, so he fully intended to do just that.

Fitting his hands around the ridge of muscle just above the waistband of Felix's sweatpants, he pushed down and let the pants drop. Felix kicked them away as Jack pivoted Felix around and kissed down the nape of his neck and across his shoulders before dropping to his knees. He'd worry about dinner later. He really had more important things to focus on at the moment.

Chapter Ten

"It's absolute bullshit, and I have half a mind to walk out and never come back."

Jack uh-huh'd and bit his lip and smiled at the lit-up screen of his phone. Felix was trying to decide on a pet name for him and kept texting ideas: *Sugar. Angel. Sweetheart. Mi Amor. Sexy. Papi.*

"Douglas! I'm having a crisis here, can you stop making moony eyes at your boyfriend's increasingly dirty nicknames and focus!"

Jack felt his face go hot. He grabbed his phone off of Lydia's desk and slid it into his pocket with a sheepish grin. "Sorry. I just miss him."

Lydia leaned forward with both elbows on her desk, which was littered with papers and fluorescent sticky notes, and dropped her cheek against a fist. "You saw him yesterday. You went for a walk in the park and had a picnic and then got ice cream, and it was so disgustingly adorable little old ladies cooed in your wake. Now. Focus."

Jack mimicked her position on his side of the desk and tried to look as serious as possible. "Okay, ready."

But she didn't laugh or roll her eyes or throw her stapler at his head; she just sighed and rubbed at her bloodshot eyes and said, "They're cutting the youth outreach program."

Jack sat up in shock. "The whole thing? Teams and camps and after school and—all of it?"

"All of it. You know, we adults need elliptical machines with built-in TV screens, but kids from impoverished neighborhoods who have nowhere else to go," she waved a hand through the air with a bitter laugh, "who cares about them?"

"Shit, Lydia. I'm sorry. Is there nothing you can do?" It was her life's work, her mission, spending so much of her time and energy making sure those kids had a positive force in their lives and now—

There was a light knock on the door, and Felix's smiling face appeared in the rectangle of window. Jack held up a finger and he nodded in reply.

Jack took Lydia's hands in his own across the messy desk. "You are so smart and so determined, and I know if anyone can figure this out it's you. And whatever you decide, I am with you one hundred percent."

And then the gloom and anger cleared from her expression and she grinned, crushing his fingers in her grip. "I was hoping you'd say that."

She let go, and Jack snatched his fingers away. He tried to shake some feeling back into them as Felix came into the office and sat down in the plastic orange chair next to Jack's.

"I asked Felix to meet us here—" Lydia began.

"Uh oh," Jack interrupted. "Not that I'm not happy to see you." He leaned in to brush a kiss to Felix's cheek, trying not to get distracted by the fact that he was obviously here post-workout; he was sweaty and musky and delectably disheveled.

But Lydia was conspiring with his boyfriend, and it was all still new and wonderful and tenuous, and Jack was pretty certain that whatever havoc Lydia was planning could not be smoothed over with a food-of-the-month club. Vodka, maybe. Sexual favors, possibly.

"Oh, calm down," Lydia chided. "I thought maybe the two of us could convince you to take on spear-heading the swimming program at the new youth center."

"What new youth center?"

Felix shrugged, and Lydia flicked her fingers impatiently. "That's still to be determined."

"So, imaginary coaching an imaginary swim team at an imaginary youth center. Sure, sign me right up," Jack said, shifting in his chair with his arms crossed defensively.

"Jack." Felix reached across to rest his hand on Jack's knee. "This could be your chance to get back into swimming. To not be stuck here."

"Not interested," Jack replied.

"Sweetie, this would be so good for you," Lydia chimed in, making that *I'm your best friend I know what's best for you* face, and here was Felix, with his ruggedly handsome yet vulnerable everything, and the kids who were facing empty homes in dangerous neighborhoods—they were right, all of them, and it was pissing him off.

Jack stood and swept papers off of Lydia's desk haphazardly until he found her laptop buried beneath the clutter. He opened it and jabbed at the keys and touchpad until he found what he'd been looking for.

"Want to know why I haven't so much as dipped a toe in a pool for years? Here you go." He spun the laptop to face Felix, crossed the room and slammed the door behind him as the echo of his own tinny, frantic, high-pitched sobs started off a viral video titled:

Olympic Hopeful MELTDOWN!

He immediately turned down the wrong hallway and went through scraping metal doors to what he expected to be the back staircase but wasn't. He was too keyed up, shaking with panic, skin crawling and cold and hands trembling. Just like that day when the buzzer sounded, and, instead of diving into the water, he'd completely lost it.

Jack stopped and pressed his clammy forehead against the whitewashed cinderblock walls across from the men's locker room. From here he could smell the chlorine, could hear the splash and lap of the water. Of course he ended up outside of the pool. He'd been treading water there for years.

His parents had found him that day and ushered him out of the pool area onto a worn wooden bench near the showers. His dad draped a towel over his shoulders and his mom soothed his hysterical, gasping breaths. They took him home and never talked about it. Not once.

He'd blown his chance. He'd collapsed under the pressure. And now he'd been telling Felix to let go, to move on, when he was the one who had let his life race past in a blur while he stood still with his heart beating frantically against his chest.

Some of his yoga students called his name in the locker room as he strode to the back, as if they were buddies meeting up at a bar. He nodded and kept moving, opened his locker and pulled out his bag: blue, with *Douglas* stitched over an American flag emblem. He dug past soft pants and a shirt made to wick away sweat, past his towel and protein bar and emergency deodorant to the little pocket in the back.

He'd never taken them out, couldn't bear it, had just pushed and pushed until he could pretend none of it had ever happened: not laughingstock Jack Douglas. Not Olympic hopeful Jack Douglas. Not swimmer Jack Douglas. He had pushed and pushed until he could pretend that person never even existed.

He closed his fist around the sleekly soft give of his suit and the hard dig of plastic and the stretching elastic on his goggles.

If he was going to take his own advice and let Felix in as Felix had done—so brave and open and surrendering—Jack knew he would have to face his own failure head-on. There was no moving forward without first taking that dive off a cliff. Or straight into the deep end.

Chapter Eleven

He stood shivering at the edge for too long, toes hanging over the starting block, breath coming shallow and quick, arms and legs rigid and cold. His form was terrible, his confidence shot. In the past he would have been reamed out for it by his coach, then spent countless hours diving over and over again, perfection dangling just out of reach every time.

A toddler swim class filled the glass-walled pool area with shrieks and splashes; the other lap lanes were empty but for two people, steadily making their way across the length and back. The air was thick with the pool chemicals that used to turn Jack's stark blond hair green when he was a little boy. The chemicals he used to be sure filled his lungs instead of oxygen.

Jack crouched, his skin crawling with goose-bumps, his fingers turned to ice. He lifted his hands to cross at the wrists in front of his head, breathed in and tried to remember what it was like when swimming was his reason for living, when he felt joy and peace and freedom as he raced through the water. He tried to remember how he had always felt a calming sense of relief after plunging under, soaring as if he was born to feel the cool caress of water currents rushing past him.

He took a breath and jumped.

On his way back to the locker room, pool water still dripping down his back and legs and chest, he nearly walked right into Felix. He was so exhilarated he felt as if he was vibrating: he had done it, gotten back in the water, and it turned out he was just fine. Better than fine. No panicking. No crushing sense of failure. Just relief.

"Jack," Felix stumbled back against the wall, clad only in a towel, holding shampoo and body wash in one hand. "Hey, about before. I shouldn't push you, and you told me not to, and—" He stopped and let his eyes travel down Jack's body. "Did you swim?"

Jack nodded, releasing a gust of breath. "I did. And—I'm glad. You were right, Lydia was right. Ugh, I hate when she's right." Jack fiddled with the goggles dangling from his neck. "I had to let go, too."

Felix curled his mouth into a slow smile. "Well, I was going to say you never had to swim again if you didn't want to. But that was before I saw you in a Speedo."

Jack pretended to fluff his drenched hair and preen. "It's not a look just anyone can pull off, this is true." He rubbed through the thatch of fair, coarse hair on his belly that would have never been allowed in a competitive setting. "Way too much waxing required, though."

Felix hummed and reached out, replacing Jack's hand with his own and stirring up a low heat that wasn't really appropriate for a YMCA locker room.

The lone running shower squeaked off and a guy exited in a cloud of steam and Irish Spring soap, walking past them and into the dressing area, out of sight.

Felix licked his lips and his irises turned even darker. "Come on."

There were no gentle caresses this time, no soft whispers or quiet connections—just Felix shoving hard against him and the cold tile against his back. Jack fumbled for the shower knobs behind him while Felix slung the plastic curtain closed with a scrape of metal rings.

They both jolted and laughed when the water came out too cold, Jack spinning to adjust it while Felix kissed along his neck and shoulders, lifted the goggles over his head and shoved his Speedo down and off in a puddle at their feet.

Jack turned again when the water was hot, found Felix's searching mouth with his own and raked his wet hair with both hands.

"If we both get athlete's foot, I'm blaming you," Jack panted out while Felix's hands groped and grabbed and pulled.

Felix reached over his shoulder to squeeze some shower gel into his cupped palm, muttered, "Don't care," against Jack's lips and gripped both of their cocks with his slick hand.

"Oh fuck," Jack groaned. Felix shushed him and laughed and twisted his wrist, so Jack clenched his jaw and clung to Felix's shoulders and let his head thunk back against the shower wall, forcing his moans to rumble like thunder through his chest.

"What was it like?" Felix asked, the head of his cock sliding and bumping against the ridge of Jack's. Jack blinked his eyes open. Beads of water blurred his vision.

"Hnng?" was all he managed to get out.

Felix grinned and slowed the pumping of his hand. "Swimming again? What was it like?"

Jack swallowed and fought the haze of lust to answer him, "Good. It was—I think I just, ahh. Just needed to see that I, uh. I still could?"

Felix grew quiet for a while. He rested his head against Jack's shoulder and watched the steady jerking of his hand, just loose and slow enough to keep Jack on the torturous, desperate edge.

"Hey," Jack rubbed Felix's back, the water a coursing river on their bodies. "Still with me?"

Felix didn't answer, but lifted his head and kissed Jack hard again.

Jack wrapped his own hand around Felix's; their slippery fingers joined and moved tightly together, the breath humid between their lips, their eyes low, watching, wanting, desire winding up tighter and faster and harder.

Jack muffled his cry against Felix's neck, bit down sharply against the muscle there and came. Felix grunted, snapped his hips and followed.

"You're amazing," Felix said after they'd sheepishly left the shower, trying not grin too hard or look too guilty, exiting the stall like secret agents. Naked secret agents.

Jack tugged his shirt over his head. "Well, you did most of the work there, but thanks."

"No, I mean—" Felix cinched his belt and sat down. He paused with his socks still balled in his hand. "Pushing past your fears. Trying again. Facing things head-on."

Jack straightened his jeans and tried to arrange his unkempt hair, still stiff with chlorine. "I couldn't have without you giving me a nudge." He closed his locker, hitched his bag over his shoulder and ran his fingers along Felix's scalp, resting his thumb on the scar.

"You make me want to be brave."

Lilah Suzanne

Chapter Twelve

"Okay, you win. Those were the most amazing omelets I've ever had." Felix slumped back against the pillows, rubbed his stomach over his T-shirt and sighed happily. "You have officially taken the title of master chef in this relationship."

Jack smiled, giddy and pleased both with the praise for his cooking and the fact that Felix had referred to them as being in a relationship so casually and matter-of-factly. He moved the breakfast tray aside and shuffled over to settle into Felix's outstretched arms.

"So I slaved over quiches and risotto and made-from-scratch ravioli and cakes and tamales for you, and all it took was a few scrambled eggs?"

Felix hummed happily and nestled into the bed, tucking Jack tighter in his arms. "Oh, no, I needed the full Jack Douglas culinary experience. Especially the desserts. A month with you and I'm probably eligible for heavyweight status." Felix rubbed up and down Jack's back, nibbling at his lips thoughtfully. "Or maybe I should try sumo wrestling instead."

Jack rolled his eyes and pushed Felix's shirt up to reveal the sharply defined muscles of his abdomen and chest. "I don't think you're quite there yet." He ducked his head to kiss from the dip between Felix's ribs to the top of his hips and then back up, pushing impatiently at Felix's shirt until he twisted to the side to strip it off, Jack not even waiting until he had settled back down on the bed before dragging his mouth all over Felix's torso.

"Eager this morning," Felix commented.

"You're one to talk," Jack replied, cupping his palm over the shape of Felix's hardening cock, hidden under the messy bunching of the covers.

"It was the omelets. Chives get me hot, never fails."

Jack chuckled into the skin pulled taut over Felix's belly button and then mouthed back up to his chest, pausing abruptly when Felix hummed with pleasure and stretched his arms up above his head.

"Whoa, what's this?"

Felix shifted onto his side and looked curiously down at Jack, who had stopped and now hovered over a large purple bruise splotched on Felix's side, at the top of his ribs.

"Oh." Felix quickly brought his arms down and scooted away from Jack. "I met with a trainer the other day. I've been doing some rounds, just as practice."

Jack frowned and sat up, reaching out to brush his fingertips over the edge of the bruise not hidden by Felix's arm and trying to shove away dark images of Felix bloody and covered with bruises, Felix lying in a hospital bed alone, Felix angry and brooding and broken.

He pulled Felix's arm away gently and pressed his hand flat over the bruise as if he could heal it, take it away, leach Felix's pain from his chest and into the cavities of his own heart.

"Why?" So he was boxing again, no big deal. He was still happy. They were still happy. And yet—why did Felix hide this from him?

Felix flinched, turning his back to Jack as he shrugged back into his shirt. Jack could see the shift in his body, the lift of his shoulders, the knot of his jaw and the way his eyes stayed fixed on the floor, even as he stood to face Jack. And Jack knew, knew before Felix even opened his mouth to say softly, "I was going to tell you. I didn't want you to worry. I'm fighting again."

"Okay." Jack threw the covers off and padded over to the other side of the bed. "To stay in shape, or—if you're stressed out again, I can help you. There are other poses that unblock negative energy—"

Felix stood and straightened his shirt. "It's not a big deal. Just an amateur competition, not even close to the level I was at before."

"Felix, you told me that you can't fight because it's too dangerous. It can't be worth it," Jack pleaded, following Felix as he walked out of the bedroom and down the hall.

"I'll be fine," Felix said shortly, and slipped on his shoes with his back turned. "I told you. I'm tired of my past defining me. I need to prove to myself that I can still do it. You of all people should get that." He turned, flicked his eyes up at Jack warily and held his hand out in the air between them. "I really was going to tell you. And I was hoping you'd come and support me."

Jack lifted his chin and shifted back on his heels, crossing both arms over his chest. "I won't watch you kill yourself, Felix."

Jack had expected a flash of anger. To see Felix morph into the person he was before, guarded and defensive and lashing out at the world. But instead Felix stared at him, his eyes rounded with regret and sorrow and sadness.

"I understand," he said flatly, before turning the doorknob and stepping away, closing the door behind him with a soft click.

Jack spent the rest of that day and the next locked in his room, moping. Then the next two days after that—and still no word from Felix. Not that Jack had taken the initiative and tried to contact him. Instead he spent hours every night winding himself into a near-panic.

Was he just a temporary distraction to Felix? A way to blow off steam before getting back to his real life? Jack had fallen hard and fast for Felix, but he'd never said it, never told Felix just how much he needed him. And now he was pushing Felix away so it wouldn't hurt so much when he left for good, because that was what Jack did, or what he used to do: self-destruct before anything else got a chance.

He'd only contacted Felix once, had sent a text in the middle of the night when he couldn't stop thinking about him and was too tired to talk himself out of it or rationalize his own insecurities.

I do get it. I'm sorry.

He hadn't expected anything back, had closed his phone and shoved it away, had curled on his side and stared at the blank wall. Until a text chimed from under his pillow.

Me too.

HE WAS IN THE MIDDLE of what could only be described as half-assed yoga—still in cobra pose, which had devolved into an excuse for him to sprawl on the floor with his face smashed into his mat—when there was tentative knock on his door and Lydia peeked her head in.

"What is the point of knocking if you're just going to come in anyway?" Jack mumbled into the floor.

"Because you would have told me to go away." She stepped over his prone body and nudged his side with her toe insistently.

Jack groaned, "You're right. Go away."

"Oh, stop moping. Come on, I have something exciting to show you."

Jack pushed up off the floor, dragged himself to his closet, slipped on his shoes and sighed, "It better be the world's biggest tub of cookie dough ice cream or I'm gonna be so mad."

Lydia said nothing, but she had that gleam in her eyes again, and Jack found himself getting curious, for once. He really never knew what would come of that look, but it was certainly always interesting. Probably more interesting than the floor, at the very least.

"Ta-da!" Lydia trilled, sweeping her hands in front of their destination—after a train to a connecting bus and a trek through what was not the best neighborhood.

"I'm not sure *ta-da* is really the best word to sum up this place. More like *yikes*. Or *ugh*," Jack replied.

It was an abandoned swimming pool with a graffiti-covered clubhouse and rusted chain-link fence, surrounded by weeds tall enough to brush Jack's stomach and probably hiding several dangerous and terrifying creatures. Snakes. Spiders. Chupacabras. The pool was dirty, covered in algae, and empty save for a puddle of thick brown water in the deep end. But it was large and well built and holding up okay, all things considered.

Vines crawled up the side of the clubhouse, a 1970s style A-frame with dirt crusting over the stucco walls and cracked and peeling paint. The windows were boarded up, and broken glass shimmered in the barren flowerbeds beneath.

"Okay, so it needs a little TLC," Lydia conceded.

"What it needs is a wrecking ball," Jack said. Lydia elbowed him. "Ow. Okay, sorry. But why are you showing me this?"

Lydia sat down on the edge of the cracked sidewalk next to the pool. "Well. It's for sale. And I'm hoping to buy it and open a youth center with my kind and generous and very handsome roommate and best friend."

"Hmm. Keep the compliments coming, and we'll see." Jack crouched to sit next to her. Gravel and loose concrete crunched under his feet.

The sky was overcast and gray, listless dark clouds casting the city in shadow. He loved teaching yoga, loved how it brought him back to a centering place where he could figure himself out again. But that time was gone; and the possibility of moving forward, of doing something that would create a positive force not just within himself but in the world outside his own head sounded kind of perfect.

Jack craned to get another look at the crumbling building and neglected, forgotten pool, shook his head at himself and said, "Okay, I'm in."

Lydia squealed and grabbed his arm and pulled him back and forth, chanting, "Thank you, thank you, thank you," until Jack managed to shake her off.

"How are you so strong?" he groaned, rubbing his arm. "And more importantly, how do we raise the money to buy this palace?"

Lydia stood, brushed off her skirt and replied, "The answer to both questions is: sheer force of will." She grabbed Jack's hand and yanked him up. "One more favor? I need you to talk to Felix."

Jack's heart thudded off-kilter. "Why?"

"Because I need him for this plan, too. And you need him, Jack. You're different with him. Good different. I've watched you walk around sort of numb for a while. Holding everything at arm's length. From the very start you haven't been like that with him. It's a good look on you. I've missed it."

Jack turned away and watched the heavy clouds drift and the traffic pass. "And what if he doesn't need me?"

Lydia moved in close and rested her head on his shoulder. "If I know anything, Jack—and I do, I really do—it's that sometimes life doesn't go the way it should, or the way you expect it to. Sometimes it explodes in your face. But if you can't get back up and drag yourself through the rubble, you'll never get anywhere."

Chapter Thirteen

He'd been hovering at the door for a solid ten minutes meaning to leave, deciding to leave, wanting to leave, only—the keys hung on the hooks by the door were a mess.

First of all, his key chains had seen better days. There was the wooden one carved in the shape of a salmon that his dad had sent from a fishing trip in Washington. One fin was broken off and one of the little black eyes had been scraped away, as though the fish was winking at everything but not at all happily. It looked fairly panicked, actually, Jack thought as he worked the ring off and tossed it to the floor.

He still had a little key chain discount card for a bookstore that had gone bankrupt years ago, and a silver key with a soda can pull tab attached that he didn't even remember acquiring, let alone what on earth it opened. A locker he'd made himself forget, maybe.

He pulled that one off too and tossed it away: a ghost he no longer felt haunted by.

And then there were Lydia's keys.

"Are you actually a prison warden in a noir film and you forgot to mention it to me?" he demanded, shaking the huge mass of keys and key chains at her.

"You caught me," she said dryly. Her hair was twisted into a messy pile on the top of her head, and she was scribbling on scraps of paper and firing off emails while downing a carton of yogurt. She glanced up and gave him a measured look, saying around the spoon still in her mouth, "Are you going or are you just planning on dicking around until it's too late?"

"I am not *dicking around*." He frowned at the heavy collection of keys in his hand and hung them back up with a sigh. "Okay, fine. Just—what should I say?"

Lydia pulled the spoon free and set it down, stood up and gave him a fond smile. "I'd probably go with the truth."

The entrance was frosted and grimy and non-descript, nestled between an expansive high-end design studio and a taco restaurant in Brooklyn. He double-checked the address on the flyer that Lydia had all but stapled to his forehead in her insistence that he at least go watch and then started up the echoing cement staircase.

As he climbed, the din from the event got louder, from a dull hum to an uproar of shouts and cheers and groans. A bell clanged loudly just as Jack rounded the corner to the main floor.

Three boxing rings were set up there, one red-floored and red-roped and right in the middle; there were two more on either side of it, blue. Around the gym, exercise bikes were pushed to the walls, their seats wrapped with silver electrical tape, foam stuffing bursting from rips in the fabric. The weight benches were scuffed and worn, and battered punching bags leaned in the corners, their heavy metal chains coiled on the cement floor like sleeping serpents.

Spectators were crammed into every space and corner where this equipment usually sat, talking, shouting and laughing, throwing mock punches and cupping their hands around commands: *Get him! Come on! Hit him!*

The place smelled like old sweat and mildew and too many bodies, and the heat and noise pressed in on Jack as he found a spot in the back next to a thick metal pillar and a round-faced teenager standing on his toes to see over the crowd.

The bell clanged and clanged, signaling the end of a fight and the start of a new one. The referee shouted numbers: Five, who must have been winning rounds since morning, and Twenty-seven. Felix.

Jack's stomach twisted itself into knots and he had to take several deep Zen breaths to calm the panicked pounding of his heart. Number Five's trainer gripped his shoulders, tightened the strap of his helmet and cuffed his chin. Felix was alone, crouched in the corner in baggy athletic shorts, helmeted and gloved, a mouth guard stretching out his lips and cheeks. His eyes were closed. Jack watched as he breathed in, sat on the floor and folded his legs with his black gloves palm-up on his knees. He breathed again: in, in. Out. Just as Jack had showed him. Lotus position. Focus. Breathe.

From across the hot, crowded gym, Jack breathed with him. In, in. Out. *Focus the energy, feel it flow through you, become part of you. Then send it out, connected, part of something bigger.*

I'm here. Jack thought, sending the message out with an exhalation. *I'm with you. I'm here.*

The bell sounded once again, and the boy next to Jack whooped and clapped and pumped his fists into the air, but Jack couldn't seem to summon the same enthusiasm. Felix and Number Five circled each other and crouched with fists raised and faces laser-focused. Every punch Number Five landed felt like a strike to the center of Jack's own chest, even though Felix held his own, even though he looked so fluid and strong up there, his movements precise and practiced.

What pained Jack most wasn't just that he was afraid Felix would get hurt, though he was; and it wasn't just that he'd hoped he could be enough for Felix—that Felix wouldn't *need* to fight—but the ache he felt when he imagined Felix thinking that

Jack was just another person who had let him down when he needed him the most.

Felix got Number Five against the ropes, landing blow after blow. Even Jack could see the difference between the two fighters: Number Five was scrappy and determined but overeager; he extended his punches too far, lunging forward and losing his footing. He was too focused on landing blows to keep his defenses up. And like a chess player, Felix anticipated his every move with strikes that were intentional, strategic.

The kid next to Jack jumped up, landing too close to Jack and pushing him into the pillar as the rest of the crowd roared and swelled. Number Five wobbled unsteadily, dripping sweat, swinging wildly now, and Felix landed a final blow that sent him to the mat. The crowd counted down: *Three! Two! One!* And the bell clanged again as the ref yanked Felix's arm up and declared him the winner.

Lydia had been right: he was sort of numb, content to be in this place of complacent calm because he couldn't deal with the depths of anger and despair. But without feeling the lows, he was missing out on the highs; and seeing the pure, radiant, triumphant joy on Felix's face, Jack realized the extent of what he'd been missing.

Number Five started to push himself up, and Felix hooked an arm around his chest, hauling him to his feet and tapping their gloves together. He said something in his ear, and Number Five nodded and grinned at Felix, the guy who had just sent him sprawling to the ground and defeated him.

Jack really did not understand boxing at all.

He shoved off the pillar, squeezing and pushing through the crowd, trying to track where Felix headed after he ducked under the ropes and went to the back of the gym. Jack followed him down a long hallway, its cinderblock walls painted bright red, and lost track of him when he guessed and took a wrong turn only to end up at a clutch of offices with flickering fluorescent lights.

Jack heard voices coming from the other direction so he followed them, past locker rooms and into a smaller changing area with one long bench down the center and a scale next to the door. There he found a boxer and an officiator doing a weigh-in and a trainer on the phone in the corner next to them; and on the bench sat Felix, packing his equipment into a duffel bag, his thin T-shirt pulled on, sweaty and flushed and silent.

"This place could really benefit from a few scented candles," Jack said. "Might mask that heady bouquet of old gym socks and sweat a bit."

Felix looked up in surprise. "You're here."

Jack moved aside as the trainer brushed past him, still hurriedly negotiating with whomever he had on the phone, and sat astride the bench facing Felix.

"Lydia dragged me to the Bronx to show me an empty pool and make me think about some stuff."

Felix's eyebrows drew together. "Is that some kind of metaphor?"

"No. Well, maybe. The point is, I've been thinking, and I figured I owe you an explanation."

Felix turned and straddled the bench, protesting, "You don't—"

Jack stopped him, resting his fingers on Felix's knees. "I do. Because I keep coming on too strong and then pulling away and I do this thing where I act like I'm some sort of wise old yogi, but I don't actually know what the fuck I'm talking about. Like I told you to deal with your shit and I couldn't even deal with mine."

"Jack, no one else in my life ever even *cared* about my shit. You cared."

Jack nodded and traced the oblong shape of Felix's kneecap, soft dark hair springing up in the wake of his fingers. "That's the whole thing, though. I care *so much* about you. And it's kind of a lot to deal with. All of my defenses are down and the thought of you getting hurt—I couldn't handle it. And I should have."

Felix gently cupped Jack's chin, lifting his face to meet his eyes. "I care about you a lot, too. And I don't need you to be some kind of Zen master, okay? Just you. You're enough." He grinned and slid his thumb up to rub over Jack's bottom lip. "More than enough, actually."

The weigh-in finished, they now had the smelly, stifling back room all to themselves. Jack leaned in and brushed a soft kiss on Felix's lips.

"I don't think you came on too strong," Felix said, leaning back again. Jack just raised his eyebrows. "Okay, you did, but you're really cute so I let it slide."

Jack kissed him again. "I hope you know I'll be working that to my advantage from now on."

Felix laughed and twisted around to finish packing away his helmet and gloves, mouth guard and towel and water bottle beaded with moisture.

"How was it?" Jack wondered. "Fighting again?"

Felix heaved the bag onto the bench between his legs. "It was... kind of weird, actually. Like I spent so much time being angry. Angry at those kids who tortured me, angry at the people who didn't do anything. Angry at myself for letting them get to me after all this time."

He considered for a moment, flicking the zipper toggle on the bag back and forth. "But today I got up there and I wasn't angry. I realized all this time I've been fighting–"

"Ghosts?" Jack finished for him.

"Yeah. Exactly." Felix released a breath. "Hard to fight, those ghosts."

"Well, they are invisible, so. Also not real."

More people came in then, another boxer post-fight, mopping up sweat and gulping down water and his trainer at his ear, giving criticism and instructions for the next battle.

"Hey, let's get out of here."

Felix stood and started to head out, stopping to bump fists with the short but hugely-muscled, dark-skinned fighter.

"Guy's good," Felix remarked. He slung his bag over his shoulder and walked to the rusting gray door under the lit-up, orange emergency exit sign. "Vasquez might take it though, if he could just focus a little more."

"Wait. You won, don't you have another fight too?"

Felix paused with his hand on the door. "Nah. Not today." He pushed the door open and blessed fresh air, clear and crisp and distinctly not reeking of armpits, washed over Jack's humid skin.

"Okay, but I planned on a whole afternoon of watching sweaty men pound on each other, and I have to say I'm kind of disappointed now."

The door led to a back alley with a dumpster and stacks of crumbling cardboard boxes. Cigarette butts littered the ground beneath their feet.

"I promise I'll make it up to you." Felix tugged him close with an arm low on his hips. In the sunshine, Felix's neck shone with sweat; and for all of Jack's complaining about the conditions in the gym, he very much wanted to lick him everywhere.

But he somehow managed to keep this to himself, for now, and didn't even make a joke about being pounded. Instead he just breathed, "Yeah, okay," and let Felix lead the way.

Lilah Suzanne

Chapter Fourteen

He got the idea at the flea market the following Saturday, when he stopped in front of the booth with all the silk and satin wares and a deep red smoking jacket caught his eye. "Do you take custom orders?" Jack asked the tiny woman whose fingers were gnarled with age and use.

It was ready by Monday. Jack folded it, passing his hand over the fine stitching and the smooth, shimmering red of the fabric. He put it gently in his bag to wait for the right moment.

He thought of Felix in action, all fluid graceful energy, no longer fighting with fear and anger buried deep, but passion and hunger.

Tuesday morning Jack woke from a restless sleep, feeling raw and alert in a way he hadn't in so long. He stretched out in the still-dark morning and felt his own powerful energy, from fingertips to toes.

Everything felt new, fresh. A weight had lifted from his shoulders that only he had put there, carrying his shame and failure around like a security blanket. He was content, before. Centered. But now he was *happy*.

Unable to sleep past dawn, he watched the ceiling of his room grow brighter by slow increments and finally gave up with a sigh and went in to the Y even earlier than usual for Senior Yoga. The locker room was quiet and still smelled of the sharp, caustic cleaner the night crew used. It was devoid of even his usual students, who were often there in the mornings for a revitalizing steam in the sauna or soothing soak in the hot tub.

He changed in the silence, with only his thoughts to keep him company.

Just you. You're enough.

And God, he wanted to be. Sweet, kind, brave Felix, who laid himself bare for Jack, saw something in Jack that he hadn't quite worked out for himself: his own compassion. His own courage. It wasn't just that he saw Felix for who he was, for what was in his heart. They saw each other. And Jack needed Felix to know, somehow, how tremendous that was, how lucky they were to find that. But all he had were his words and his touch, and a gift meant as a symbol of his loyalty.

Jack was halfway out of his T-shirt, head stuck and one arm trapped in a sleeve, when his phone chimed and buzzed and he blindly dug it from his pocket, fumbled it and cursed and nearly dropped it onto the concrete floor, *shit, shit, shit.*

A cryptic text from Felix:

Come to yoga studio asap. Bring Lydia.

Jack jumped up, started to walk out of the locker room and then stopped with a squeak of his shoes when he realized his locker was still wide open. He ran back, slammed it shut and ran off again, only to turn and dart back to open it once more. He grabbed his bag and hesitated for just a moment before slipping the strap onto his shoulder and banging his locker closed a final time.

He sent a text to Lydia on the way. She replied:

????????

When he made it to the studio he was out of breath and just as confused as Lydia's text indicated, because the entire Senior Yoga class was gathered there. Including Felix, who took one look at Jack and lit up like sunlight after a storm, so shockingly bright Jack thought he'd have to shield his eyes.

"Hi," Jack breathed.

Felix came closer, and when he was within arm's reach Jack pulled him in—couldn't not, needed to feel him again, to breathe him—and gripped Felix's shirt in his hands and held him.

"Hi yourself."

"Okay, okay. Save the mushy stuff for later," Murray said, earning a dirty look from Jan.

Lydia came in, her face scrunched in confusion. "What's going on?"

Felix moved away, but his fingers lingered on Jack's arm and his hand passed with a flutter over

117

the jut of his hip. "So, Lydia and I were in contact while we were fi—uh. Figuring stuff out."

Jack whipped his head around and raised his eyebrows at Lydia, who suddenly became very interested in the ceiling vents.

"She told me more about the pool and clubhouse and I got to talking to some of the guys in the sauna the other day-"

"Your boy's in great shape. Well done," Murray chimed in. And Jack really had no response for that, true as it was.

"Um. Thanks," Felix pressed on. "Anyway. I had an idea and—here." He pulled a folded rectangle of paper from his pocket and pressed it into Jack's hand while Lydia leaned over to see and made a hysterical sort of gasping sound.

"Felix, how did you get all this money?" It was enough to cover the down payment and then some, certainly enough to get the youth center up and running.

"Everyone pitched in, and even the smallest donations were a huge help," he said, turning back to the group with a warm look. "And the money I would have used for a trainer... plus what's left of the winnings from my championship."

"You stopped training? Felix, you can't give up just because I—" Jack turned the check over and over in his hands. He needed Felix to know. "I can't take your dream away from you," Jack said shakily, his chest tight, his eyes starting to blur. Not when he could finally admit how awful it was to have a dream ripped away. Not when he had seen for himself the way Felix came alive in a boxing ring.

But Felix shook his head. "I don't need it anymore. This is a fresh start for you and Lydia and those kids. And for me, too."

He folded Jack's fingers over the check and held his hand tightly. "Someone much wiser than me once told me that dreams change. My dream changed. It never had you in it before."

"Felix," Jack breathed.

"Of course he also quoted Suzanne Somers once, so his wisdom may be questionable."

"Thank you," Jack said, to Felix and then to all the others. He flushed with warmth and gratitude and relief, pressed a hand to his heart and smiled, and headed to the corner to retrieve the mats for class. "But if you all think your amazing kindness and generosity is gonna make me go easy on you, you can forget it."

He caught a glimpse of Lydia wiping her eyes and hugging Felix, and Jack's heart fluttered warmly when he saw the two of them press their foreheads together and whisper, these two people who meant so much to him, who never gave up on him. Who cared enough to keep fighting for him.

While his students organized themselves, Jack retrieved his bag from where he'd dropped it in the corner by the door. He unzipped it and pulled out Felix's gift.

119

"I have something for you, too," he said, shaking the fabric open and holding it up with outstretched arms.

Felix tipped his head. "A boxing robe?"

"I just—I want you to know I'm in your corner," Jack said with an awkward chuckle, even though he meant every word. "I support you, whatever you decide."

Felix draped the red satin robe over his arm and brushed a kiss on Jack's cheek. "Thank you. You know, I'm really glad I made a mistake and ended up in Yoga for Seniors. And here I thought that would be the last place I'd find love."

The flutter in Jack's chest turned hummingbird frantic and threatened to fly free of his chest. "I love you, too," he said, trying to tamp down his elation and failing utterly.

"Sometimes our mistakes lead us to our destinies," Felix said solemnly, taking Jack's hand again and breaking into an impish grin that made Jack want to pinch his side and then kiss him everywhere.

Jack lifted his eyes to the ceiling and groaned. "God, how obnoxious was I? No wonder you stormed out of my class."

He looked back down and ran his thumb over the top of Felix's hand. "I'm glad I found you again, though." Jack wrinkled his nose. "Kept finding you. Sort of accidentally stalking you… "

"I love that you care so much." Felix squeezed his hand tight. "It's not a bad thing."

Jack cleared his throat and tried for a joking tone, but he still had a nagging insecurity. "So I didn't just eventually wear you down, then?"

"Jack, you are wonderful and kind and utterly charming." Jack blushed and made sounds of protest. Felix ducked his head and batted his eyes shyly. "Or at least that's the story we should tell our family and friends, because honestly I was less motivated by that and much more by the fact that you have a really fantastic ass."

Jack wiggled his hips, and then his eyebrows. "Well, I can't fault you for that."

"Really, though." Felix said. "Not many people have taken the time to get to know me, the real me. And you were so patient, and willing to be so available and flexible, and I know it wasn't easy—"

"It was worth it," Jack replied emphatically.

"Thank you," Felix replied, his voice going thick. He brushed soft kisses across the knuckles of Jack's hand.

"And Felix?"

"Mmmm?"

"You have no idea just how flexible I am."

Lilah Suzanne

Chapter Fifteen

Of all the new skills he'd learned in the months spent getting the center ready—through blood, sweat, tears and a lot of colorful language—maintaining the pool chemicals was, pretty ironically, one of Jack's least favorite. It placed somewhere below pulling weeds and scrubbing algae by hand, but still ranked above snaking a toilet. And the less said about the discovery of what had been clogging the toilet, the better. It haunted his dreams as it was.

Jack pulled the test strip from the water. Sunlight reflected, dazzling, on the crystal surface and beat down relentlessly on his back where he hunched over the edge of the pool, surrounded by bottles and containers labeled DANGER and TOXIC and KEEP AWAY FROM CHILDREN in scary red letters. "I spent most of my life marinating in this shit. I'm starting to worry I may be slightly brain damaged."

"Slightly?" Lydia smirked from the metal bleachers behind him, legs crossed in front of her. She was covered in paint splatters from head to toe after the final, last-minute touch-ups.

Felix made a choked-off snorting sound next to him. Jack turned and waved the little test stick in his face. "Oh, you're agreeing with her?"

Felix stayed focused on his task—stretching rainbow-colored lane lines across the pool—pursed his lips and said, "I'm staying out of it, as usual." Then he hooked the rope securely, stood and moved on to the next one.

Jack was only distracted for moment by the bulge of Felix's arms as he heaved the ropes in place, by the tight tendons in his neck and his skin, bronzed and glistening. Or at least until Lydia announced, "One hour until we open for the first time!"

The he managed to tear his gaze away and finish his chemistry experiment.

By the time the doors opened and people began to trickle in, all three of them were exhausted, soaked with perspiration and very likely smelled terrible. But the turnout was great, the sign-up sheet filled quickly, and the mood was so enthusiastic and ebullient and triumphant that Jack half expected someone to hand him a trophy and blue ribbon.

"Great job, team," Lydia said later outside the center, the sky turned an inky blue and stars winking on, the heat of the day giving way to a cool, clear evening. "I'd high-five you, but I don't think I can lift my arms."

"A high-five in spirit," Felix smiled sweetly, setting his hand on Jack's lower back as they all proudly admired their work.

The pool was clear and blue and the water lapped gently against its whitewashed sides. The fence had been replaced; the grass around it was clipped and green and dotted with bright bursts of flowers.

The graffiti was covered, the vines gone, the windows replaced. Shutters and doors and drainpipe were painted over, shingles repaired, rubble cleared. But Jack's very favorite part was the mural on the wall facing the main road that all the kids in the program had helped to paint: A yellow and orange sun with a sharp periwinkle sky and a rainbow, the words *"Champion Youth Center. Mind. Body. Community."* painted underneath.

"Oh hell, screw high-fives," Jack said, gathering Lydia and Felix into his arms and holding them both tight.

"Okay, okay," Lydia ducked out of the hug, wiping her eyes and sniffling. "I love you both dearly but I need a shower and wine and bed, in that order. Good night."

"Mmm, a shower sounds like a great idea," Felix said after she'd gone, the two of them snuggled together and quiet. He moved closer to slide his mouth down Jack's throat, the scraggly beard he'd been sporting the last couple weeks catching roughly on Jack's skin.

Jack shivered. "I guess Lydia does have some pretty good ideas."

The first few months had come off with only a few hiccups and minor mishaps. Kara the evil trainer turned out to have a soft spot for kids and volunteered to run the fitness programs. Local businesses donated furniture and equipment and supplies.

Murray's granddaughter—the accountant with the childbearing hips—offered to help them with the books. And Murray himself, along with most of the others from the Yoga for Seniors class, came by often to mentor and volunteer, sitting with the kids at the tables in the front for summer—and soon after-school—tutoring, or on the couches in the back, telling stories.

"Mr. Murray is hilarious. All my grandpa does is complain about the government and take naps," said Ike, a tall, skinny kid with a loud laugh and soft voice.

"He's a riot, all right." Jack checked Ike out of the system for the day and stood to lean over the tall desk at the entrance. "I'll see you at the meet on Saturday, eight o'clock sharp."

Ike groaned and pulled his ball cap down.

"I know, I know. But it's the last meet of the season and we need you. With that backstroke of yours, the East Park Swim Club won't know what hit them."

Ike rolled his eyes and mumbled a goodbye, but Jack could see the smile fighting to break free on his face and the delighted gleam in his eyes.

It was a look he saw on his kids a lot. And one that never failed to make his whole week: pride.

The center was emptying for the day, with just a few stragglers waiting for their parents to pick them up and a couple of neon-haired girls still on the back couches after the LGBT teen support group had ended, talking in hushed voices and holding hands.

Jack felt a rush of warmth as he passed them, and then that deep feeling of contentment that came over him, every time—even now, one incredible year later—Felix came into view.

The boxing program had become their shining star; there was a waiting list, and they'd had a write-up in a local independent newspaper and a fluff piece on the local news. Felix had a group of junior lightweights gathered around him like a clutch of fuzzy ducklings, all skinny limbs and knobby knees and boxing gloves as big as their heads cinched to their hands.

Jack pulled himself up by a rope, hung his arms over the ring and watched.

" ...Never to be used for fighting at school or to torture your little sister. What we're focusing on here is respect and discipline and focus," Felix was saying, the kids' rounded, solemn eyes drinking in every word, every move, as though Felix himself had gone up and pinned every star in the sky. Jack could relate.

"If you just go in with fists flying you're going to lose, every time. Just remember that your greatest weapons are here." He touched his glove to his temple, the one with the scar that had mostly faded into a soft, smooth line that Jack sometimes felt under his fingertips. Felix looked at Jack, smiled in that way that always made the world tilt around them, just a bit, and touched his glove to his heart. "And here."

THEY CLEANED UP, shut off the lights and locked the doors once all the kids were gone, leaving a reminder on the desk for Lydia to clear out the tables and chairs for Jack's morning yoga class when she opened tomorrow so Jack could snag an extra blissful twenty minutes of sleep in the morning.

He stuck the note on the dark computer screen and waited for Felix at the front door so they could leave and maybe have some time for an actual date. He propped his hip on the door frame and crossed his arms. They both spent so much time here, and yet it seemed they were always somehow just passing each other by.

"Hey, how about some sushi?" Jack called as Felix made his way over after vacuuming the back.

"Sounds great." Felix stood the vacuum in the corner, wound the cord and came over; but instead of pushing open the door for Jack as usual, he hesitated, hands in his pockets and his shoulders rounded. "Or maybe... something different?"

Jack felt a cool twist of nerves in his gut. Was something wrong? Was Felix fed up with them hardly getting to spend any time together? Had he been faking since their first day and didn't actually like sushi at all? Jack pushed off from the door frame, bracing himself.

"I was… " Felix rubbed the back of his neck and laughed nervously. "I was actually hoping maybe you'd want to move some stuff in tonight." He pulled one hand out of his pocket, opening his fist to reveal a bronze key on a key chain that looked like a mini-boxing glove.

Jack's face drew tight in confusion. "What is—"

"It's a key to my place. I was, uh—I mean, we both work for a nonprofit now and it doesn't really pay much and we should be practical and my place is closer. And I know it's small, but you've always seemed to like it and—"

"Felix." Jack plucked the key from his hand and laced their fingers together. "I'd love to."

"Really?" Felix beamed and swung their joined hands. "That's great! So great. Hey, in the future, feel free to stop my nervous rambling right away."

Jack led them out of the center, sliding the locks into place and shoving against the door to test them. He struggled for moment to get his new key on his key ring. "Aww, I like your nervous rambling. It's cute."

Felix narrowed his eyes and then turned his expression to a wide-eyed pleading. "Okay, since I'm so cute and all, will you cook one of your amazing dinners in our apartment tonight instead of us going out? And that way, you know. The bed is right there. Just saying."

"Oh I see," Jack replied. The sky swirled in pinks and oranges as the sun went down and they walked to their bus stop. "You just want me to move in with you to cook and service you sexually. Well let me tell you something, mister." He stopped and turned and poked a finger into Felix's chest. "I am totally on board."

Felix laughed and tugged him in for quick kiss. "Not at all. Actually, I realized that my life is totally different from what I expected it to be, and it's more perfect than I ever imagined." He slid his arm around Jack's waist and rested it, his eyes so dark and serious they stole Jack's breath from his lungs.

"And the only thing that would make it more perfect," he continued in a husky voice, "would be falling asleep next to you every night and waking up next to you every morning."

Jack's breath hitched and he looked at Felix. He felt so lucky, so grateful that he'd been willing to try and keep trying. "I'm so in love with you," he said.

Felix pressed the softest of kisses to Jack's lips. "I'm so in love with you, too."

They headed down the sidewalk again, holding hands tightly. Jack looked over at Felix and said, "Can we at least keep the sex slave idea on the table? Just as an option."

Felix ducked his head and huffed a laugh, his arm solid around Jack's waist where their bodies curved to meet. He wisely didn't answer; Jack hummed, kissed his warm temple and stayed close in his arms as the fading sun glowed from behind the clouds and they walked home—and wherever life took them after that—together.

Lilah Suzanne

Acknowledgments

This book would not exist without the brains and brawn behind Interlude Press, so I'd like to thank them first, for seeing something in me that I very much hope I can live up to. I'd like to thank my husband for his steadfast, if slightly perplexed, support. My parents for always, always encouraging me, even when I didn't want to hear it. Especially then. My sisters and my best friend for already knowing what I could do and waiting patiently for me to realize it. And I'd like to acknowledge every single person who has liked, commented, reblogged or quietly supported something I've written. You are the reason this story exists and the reason I am still writing. I will never be able to express the depths of my gratitude to all of you for giving me that gift. I hope this is a start.

interlude press

A Reader's Guide
to
Pivot and Slip

Reader's Guide

1. How do dreams and passion, both the pursuit and loss of both, emerge as an overriding theme of the story?

2. What types of strength, both mental and physical, are explored?

3. Without boxing Felix feels a loss of identity and worth. How does Jack help him find himself again?

4. The yoga *Om,* a chant or mantra of taking in energy, centering oneself, then connecting to the energy around us, is a major part of yoga. How does this concept relate to Jack's journey? How does he use it to connect with Felix and help him with his past?

5. Jack and Felix are both haunted by the ghosts of their pasts, Felix with anger and Jack with denial. Is this an inherently bad thing? Should bad experiences always be left behind, or is there a way to connect them to the present and future in a positive way?

6. Lydia is a very driven, determined person who takes helping others very seriously. Jack frequently calls her meddling, but how vital was she to Jack and Felix's happy ending?

7. A sense of abandonment is woven throughout *Pivot and Slip*. The elderly people Jack teaches. The

disadvantaged youth that Lydia works with. Jack's swimming. The community center and empty pool. Felix being deserted by people he thought were in his corner. How do these abandoned places and people and things become a nexus where hope and love spring anew?

8. How are breathing and breath used as important transitions in the plot?

9. How is the title *Pivot and Slip* a theme of the story? How does it relate to boxing? To falling in love? To chasing dreams?

10. Both Felix and Jack are involved in very intense, high-pressure individual sports. How does this story explore the pressure put on young athletes and the repercussions of such intense drive and focus at early ages?

Coming In 2015

Spice

by
Lilah Suzanne

Magazine columnist Simon Beck spends his days masquerading as a sex and relationship expert, but his own love life is a mess. The guy he's been pining after remains aloof and unattainable, his best friend is getting ready to marry the love of her life, and Simon is starting to think that the most meaningful relationship he'll ever have is the one he has with his dog.

Until the morning his computer won't start and a sweet, gorgeous IT specialist named Benji swoops in to fix Simon's busted processing unit, and maybe his heart. Can Simon set aside his notions of an idealized perfect relationship and let Benji in, or will his fears get the best of him?

Chapter One

Ask Eros: Dangling On The Hook

I've been with this guy for almost a year and we have a lot of fun together. The sex is great and we hang out at my apartment all the time. He's met my friends and family. The problem is I know almost nothing about his life. He won't let me meet his friends, claiming they won't like me. He says he's not close to his family but he goes home all the time. We don't go out on dates. We aren't even Facebook official. Not even "it's complicated." Should I push the issue and ask him to commit? I think a year has been long enough for him to figure out what he wants.

Dear Dangling:

Instead of trying to suss out what he wants and thinks and needs, why not spend more time on what you want. Which is not, I'm guessing, a guy who thinks so little of you that he won't take you out and show you off to his friends and family and the greater world at large. Because the thing is, that's is exactly what you should get. And nothing less. Spending a year with a guy who wants to keep you hidden away and confused is 364 days too long. Time to get off that hook and swim away to bigger and better things, little fish.

spice *(excerpt)*

* * *

Simon pats his face with a damp paper towel, the automatic sink clunking on and off every time he leans into the mirror. A toilet flushes; a man in a crisp suit comes out and adjusts his tie, checks his teeth and leaves without washing his hands. Simon watches him go with a shudder.

He tosses the paper towel into the gleaming silver trashcan (who knew trash cans could be so elegant) and takes a deep breath. His hair is standing up in the back, that whorl that seems determined to defy gravity no matter how much he spends on hair product. His pants need tailoring, but he'd bought the outfit in a bit of a rush.

The bathroom attendant watches him, arms crossed and leaning against the marble sink. Another man comes out, washes his hands, takes a paper towel, but doesn't leave a tip. The attendant sighs and uncrosses and re-crosses his arms, resumes his position against the lip of the counter. Simon digs in his pocket, flips open his wallet and takes out some bills.

He's not sure how much to tip someone who stands in the men's room of a swanky five-star hotel all day passing out paper towels and mints. And what leads to such a career choice anyway? Is the guy upwardly mobile? Does he someday want to own a bathroom attendant empire across Manhattan and the outer boroughs?

Simon stuffs the money into the jar to a grunted *thanks bruh* and then checks the time on his phone. Okay, he's officially stalling now.

"Do I look like a man who's ready for a serious, committed relationship to you?"

The guy has thick black-rimmed glasses that he probably doesn't need, a piercing through the middle of his nose and an eighties-era Flock-Of-Seagulls-style haircut that Simon desperately hopes is meant to be ironic, with *Toph* labeled on his name tag.

He never uncrosses his arms or moves from his position, but obliges Simon with a quick once over. "Nope."

Simon frowns down at his outfit, too-big slacks and a dress shirt still stiff and starchy, topped off with a Ralph Lauren tie. The overall effect is less epic love story and more Episcopalian-heading-to-Sunday-services, now that he looks closer at it. "It's the tie, right? I knew the tie was too much."

"Nah, man," Toph says, still unmoving. "It's like—you look miserable. Love should lift you up where you belong, you know what I'm saying?"

Simon opens his mouth to argue, but Toph looks well-past bored with the conversation, so he just sighs and opens the bathroom door with an elbow. He's just nervous. That's all. Andrew finally invites him out, to a beautiful, fancy hotel even, and it's just been quick lunch dates so far, but Simon knows Andrew has feelings for him. Or— He thinks so. It's hard to tell what Andrew wants.

On the elevator to the top floor, he yanks the tie loose enough to pull over his head, can feel the cowlick getting even worse, stuffs the tie in his pocket and bounces on the balls of his feet.

His palms are clammy, and his pulse races too hard against his throat. The ride up feels endless; people getting off and on and barely sparing him a glance. He's out of place and uncomfortable, he's sure everyone can tell; last minute Andrew calls when Simon is already tucked into bed, says he needs Simon, and aren't those the words he's been waiting to hear? So if this is what it takes to show Andrew that he's serious, that they should be serious, then this is what he has to do.

Simon stares at the heavy door of the hotel room for slightly too long, then knocks just once before Andrew pulls the door open, sleeves of his dress shirt rolled up, blazer discarded on the king-size still-made bed. He's on the phone. He beckons Simon in with a nod, then walks to the side of the room with two chairs and a handsome oak table strewn with papers and wide window covered with heavy curtains pulled tight.

Simon sits on the very edge of the bed, hands folded and tucked between his knees, trying to ignore whatever Andrew is saying on the phone in a hushed, placating tone.

"Yeah. I've got it covered," Andrew says at normal volume, tapping his phone to end the call and turning to Simon on the bed. "Advertising. So needy. Anyway, thanks for coming."

"I—sure. I was just hanging out at home anyway—"

"Great. Great. Listen, sorry we couldn't meet at my place. I'm repainting."

It sounds like a flimsy excuse, not that Simon minds the hotel. He was actually expecting a little wining and dining room-service style, or maybe— "Do you want to go down to the bar? I could use a drink," Simon says with a small laugh.

Andrew sits next to him, the bed dipping so they're close enough that Simon can feel the heat of his body, the scent of cedar and pepper from Andrew's cologne. Their knees brush and Andrew smiles and then—his phone chimes with a text.

Andrew pats his knee once, then stands to retrieve his phone. Simon releases a shaky breath.

"Shit."

"Everything okay?" Simon croaks out. He really could use a drink. Or two. Or several.

"Yeah, just. I'm sorry, I've got someone on the way; we're gonna have to do this quickly."

Simon blinks, frozen in his perch on the edge of the bed. Andrew peels the suspenders from his shoulders, heads to a drawer in the nightstand and digs around in it for a moment as Simon watches. Andrew is the epitome of Simon's ideal partner: blond and average height, classically handsome and put together, just what he imagined he'd find when he moved to New York and found his place. Simon has wanted this since his first day at *Ravish* magazine, has wanted him.

Andrew returns to the bed and Simon stands, ready, ready to be whatever Andrew needs him to be and—

"Here."

Simon frowns at Andrew's outstretched hand, a small blue flash drive in his open palm. Simon takes it. "What's this?"

"A flash drive. Oh fuck, you do know how to use one don't you?" As Andrew runs a hand over his face, Simon notices shadows of stubble and dark circles under his eyes—something Simon's never seen in the years he's worked with him at the magazine. He's never looked like anything less than perfect.

"Yeah, of course. But— Why?"

"I need you to organize all of those spending reports, see if anything unusual crops up and make a note of it, then call me immediately so we can discuss it."

Andrew folds his fingers over Simon's, pressing the flash drive hard into his skin—sharp cold corners and Andrew's strong hands.

"Okay... Don't you have accountants for that? I thought we— I thought this was—"

Andrew's phone chimes again. He drops Simon's hand, grips him by the arms. "I need you for this, Simon. I know you have the time—"

"I'm a writer. I have time for writing." Simon interrupts.

Andrew steps back, scrubs his hands through his hair, making a mess of its perfect part. "You give women advice about what dildos to buy. I'm sure you can find room in your schedule." He picks up his phone, fires off a text. Simon's jaw clenches and he fights off the rise of defensiveness sitting sick in his gut. It's true, after all.

"I'm actually working on an exposé about a school superintendent accepting bribes..." Simon tries weakly. He isn't, not lately anyway. Because it's boring, and he likes the stuff he writes, even if it is pointless fluff. He slips the flash drive in his pocket.

Andrew isn't listening. "Hey, that's great!" He finishes texting, drops his phone on the high-thread count duvet. "So you can do that for me, then?"

He brushes fingers along Simon's hip, just enough stir up the familiar heat in Simon's veins that he can never quite help when Andrew looks at him like that.

Simon swallows. "Sure."

He's bustled out as quickly as he was bustled in, the door closing behind him before Simon can get his head around what just happened. He shuffles down the long hallway to the elevator, the ding greeting him just as he arrives.

A cute young brunet gets off, all of eighteen or so, in pants so tight he must have spray painted them on, looking at his phone and brushing past Simon. The doors slide shut before Simon can be sure, but he swears the kid stops in front of Andrew's room.

He's out in the cool, busy night before he realizes he lost his tie somewhere. It was his only one, too. And by the time he makes it back to his apartment, not only is he too tired and out of sorts to write anything, he's completely missed a *Friends* marathon— and he forgot to set his DVR to record. Simon kicks his shoes off into his tiny closet, bangs it closed, throws his keys and wallet and phone on the Formica countertop and sheds his uncomfortable slacks and dress shirt.

Walt looks up from his bed with a sleepy glance, whaps his skinny tail against the bed twice, then goes back to sleep.

"Don't get too excited, Walt. It's just me." He flops down next to the dog, turns the TV on to Gordon Ramsay yelling about something. At least the night isn't a total wash.

"I didn't even get laid," Simon groans. Walt sighs. He gets it. Simon will get to those spending reports later, or maybe call and try talk to Andrew about them. But for now he snuggles up to the only guy who's ever there for him, even if he does smell as if he rolled in something that's been dead for weeks, and watches other people's screw-ups for a little while.

Chapter Two

Ask Eros: No Scrubs

Lately my boyfriend hasn't really been in the mood for sex, but I guess he's still in the mood for porn because I can hear him watching it. To make matters worse he's leaving stains from when he…You know. Finishes. It's ruining my couch. Any tips for getting rid of them?

Dear No Scrubs:

I think you mistyped. Any tips for getting rid of him? That's what you meant, right? You don't need me to tell you that you deserve better, but here it is anyway: You deserve better. At the very least, you deserve someone who wants you and respects you enough be honest or at the very, very least to clean up after himself. Or just uses some tissues for god's sake; it's not that hard. But for now, tell him to use cold water and Oxyclean. Blot, don't scrub. Then kick that scrub to the curb.

* * *

He wakes before his alarm the next morning to whining and a wide, wet tongue licking at the arm stretched back under his pillow.

"Walt, we seriously need to have a talk about your armpit fetish," Simon grunts, shoving the dog away until he jumps off the bed, then runs back and forth from the bedroom to the front door until Simon finally relents, drags himself out of bed and yanks on sweats just as his phone gives its first cheery wake-up call.

Outside, the city hints at new life, new beginnings: trees dotted with green buds, birds chattering from electrical wire perches and the air crisp with fresh flowers growing in window planters and for sale from carts parked on the sidewalk. He turns toward the park, Walt tugging at his leash, ears flapping and tongue lolling from the side of his mouth as Simon dodges people and darts through traffic.

After a quick stop for coffee, they make it to the fenced-in area where Simon can let Walt loose and watch him bound away to chase butterflies or roll in excrement of some sort. He sits on the bench and catches up on emails, pages through some of the questions submitted for this week's column and sips his mocha.

"Is that a pit bull?" An older woman sits next to him, one of those tiny yappy dogs tucked under one arm.

"He's a mix actually. But yeah, mostly." He shuts off his phone and pockets it with a sigh. No messages from Andrew. Several *Ask Eros* submissions that can be boiled down to someone's asshole boyfriend being an asshole. Suddenly two shots of espresso are not nearly enough to deal with this day.

"Aren't you worried about how dangerous he is?" The woman whispers, as if Walt will overhear and remember he's supposed to be going on a murderous rampage.

Simon searches the grass, finds Walt digging a hole, then shoving his nose in said hole and covering his entire face in mud. "No, not really."

In fact, Simon is starting to think that Walt is the only decent living being in the entire city.

They get back, Walt tuckered out for now, and Simon just starting his day. He eats a bowl of granola and blueberries and yogurt, shaves and showers. When he jerks off under the warm spray, he tries to think of Andrew. Handsome, successful Andrew with his appropriately sized muscles and classic features. But the picture in Simon's head keeps morphing into blurry anyone-else men. When he comes with a shudder, it just feels kind of empty and disappointing.

Dressed in a soft, thin, gray sweater, skinny fit twill pants and black and white checked classic Vans, Simon feels more like himself. Not whatever he was trying to be last night. He gathers up the stiff dress shirt and boxy pants, only remembering the flash drive when it clatters to the bottom of the hamper. He hesitates for a moment, then puts it in his pocket. He said he would help. And he tries to be honest, he does.

A text comes in just as he's settling in to work at the office, dropping the flash drive into a drawer as he sits in his desk chair and starts his computer.

Tia: How did last night go?
Simon: It didn't.
Tia: Sorry :(Want to come to my office and talk about his pretentious taste in music?
Tia: Seriously if he tells me about a 'hot new jazz dive' one more time…
Simon: No I have to get working on my column. Cocktails later?
Tia: Like you have to ask.

Simon takes a deep breath, stretches his arms behind him and waits for the desktop to boot up. Only it isn't making its usual wheezing and whirring sounds. The screen is blank. Just the fan is running, hard and loud as it does when he's been streaming hilarious animal videos, listening to music and researching something all at the same time.

"Come on." He turns it off. Back on. Hits the unit under his desk and curses at it, as if either of those things will help. Nothing. He puts in a call to IT.

"Is nine in the morning too early for vodka?" Simon slumps into a chair, straightens the *Tia Robinson, Features Editor* name plate on the desk.

"Wow, that bad?" Tia looks away from her computer screen, fingers still clacking away. He has no idea how she does that. Most of his first drafts are barely legible when he *is* looking at them.

Simon sits up a bit. "Just one of those days, you know?"

Tia watches him for a moment, then finally looks back to whatever she was working on.

"Can I ask you something?"

"I think you just did."

She taps at the keyboard, dark brown eyes flitting to his for a brief moment. "Why am I friends with you again?"

"Because I'll take you out for cocktails at nine in the morning?" Simon offers.

"Right." She looks at him fully now, stops working, hands pressed flat to her desktop. "Why are you so hung up on Andrew anyway? He's decent looking and all, but. Kind of a tool, honestly," she says, which is... kind of an understatement.

"I dunno. I've put so much work into it. You know I hate to leave a project unfinished," he jokes, but Tia doesn't laugh.

"A relationship shouldn't be a project."

Simon shrugs, looks away to the stack of bridal magazines and binders full of seating charts and catering companies, menus and color schemes and flower meanings. Easy for her to say, when she's getting ready to marry the tall, dark and handsome love of her life who worships the ground she walks on.

"I just thought I'd be there by now. My happy ending."

"Well, maybe he's just around the corner," she says, then looks up and over his shoulder. "Speaking of around the corner, there's IT."

Simon wrinkles his nose, "Is it the one with the weird goat beard?" The one who smelled like pork rinds and whose nose whistled on every inhale and who drove Simon so crazy that he had to leave to get a third cup of coffee and then spent the rest of the day jittery and unfocused.

"No, it's the cute one."

"There's a cute one? Why was I not informed that there's a cute one?"

Simon pushes up from his chair, gives Tia a look that he hopes accurately portrays his feeling of betrayal, and heads back to his cubicle.

At first glance cute IT guy is a little scruffy looking, shaggy copper-red hair and wearing a T-shirt and worn jeans. But as Simon approaches, he can appreciate how well the T-shirt fits his long body—strong, lean muscle over fair, freckled skin. Gorgeous gray-blue eyes, a jawline and cheek bones that make Simon want to groan out of both jealousy and sexual frustration.

Simon's eyes drop, just a glance. Great ass. God, he's striking. Where has IT been hiding this guy?

A vast improvement over nose-whistling-strange-goatee-dude.

Simon clears his throat, manages to get ahold of himself. He has got to get laid. "Hey, you must be from tech support? We talked on the phone earlier?"

"Yeah, I'm Benji." He holds his hand for Simon to shake—good grip, bright smile.

"Simon," He scoots into the cubicle past Benji and attempts to turn the computer on again. "So it won't start, basically. And yes, it's plugged in."

Benji smiles, but it's not mocking. It's kind. "I'll go ahead and assume you weren't using the disk drive as a cup holder?"

Simon presses the "on" button repeatedly, slides Benji a look. "Seriously?"

"True story." He sits at Simon's desk chair, shoulder gently brushing Simon's hip, and Simon assumes it's because his love life has settled into a barren and frigid ice age that the contact sends a thrill coursing through his body.

He moves to the side to give Benji room to work; he types some codes and commands but the screen stays stubbornly blank. As he works Simon watches his biceps bulge under the sleeves of his worn blue T-shirt, which has a familiar emblem.

"Captain America?" Simon asks with a nod.

"Hmm?" Benji looks up, then tugs at his shirt, pulling it away from his neck and revealing the hollow scoop of a collarbone. "Oh. Yeah. I guess I've kind of had this shirt forever." He gets up to pull the processing unit out from under the desk. "I think it might be the motherboard, but I'll have to take it apart to be sure."

"Of course." Simon sighs. Benji gives an apologetic smile. "So, why Captain America?"

He ducks under the desk, pulls a tiny screwdriver from his little tool set and focuses on removing the back of the unit. "Um. I guess I just liked the idea of a good guy who does the right thing just because it's the right thing to do?" He's almost completely under the desk, just his head popping out behind the CPU.

"That makes sense."

Benji gives an awkward, hunched-over shrug. "And, you know. Nerdy redheaded gay kid. Guess I liked imagining there was someone out there who would think I was worth fighting for. It made me feel like everything would be okay."

"I always kind of liked Spiderman myself," Simon muses. "But I just thought he was cool."

Benji pokes his head out again, the insides of the computer now exposed. "You do kind of have a Peter Parker thing going on."

Simon snorts. "Pre-radioactive bite, though. Like before he turns into a super stud."

Benji gives him a once over, eyes shifting blue-gray to green-gray in the shadow of the desk. "I always thought he was hotter before the bite. Too full of himself after."

Despite being a grown man who gives sex advice for a living, Simon finds his face flushing hot and something akin to a giggle escaping his mouth. That, of course, is the moment Andrew chooses to stop by his cubicle.

"Simon. Dinner." He leans against the opening, points with a raise of his eyebrows.

Simon spins his chair, glancing down at Benji, who's hidden from view, and for the first time, he hesitates. "I made plans with Tia, and then I need to get home to walk Walt."

Andrew crosses his arms over his chest; he's in yet another high-end suit that looks pretty much like all of his other high-end suits. "Walt?"

"My dog. You know I have a dog, Andrew." Simon says.

"Well, the dog can wait and Tia will understand. Come on. Trendy new artisanal place. You love that stuff."

He steps into the cubicle, closer and closer until Simon's chair is trapped between him and the desk. Andrew brushes his fingers down Simon's arm, circles his fingers around Simon's wrist like the tight clamp of a cuff.

"Come on."

"Okay, fine." Simon relents.

Andrew beams, triumphant. "Great." He leaves the cubicle and heads back his office, but then turns on his heel to say loudly, "Did you bring a change of clothes? Or are you really wearing that?"

Simon stares after him, wonders why, when he opens his mouth to say *no* or better yet, *fuck off*, what always comes out is *yes*. Why is he so hung up him? Is it really just the lack of better offers?

"Friend of yours?" Benji asks, still shadowed under the desk.

Simon pulls his feet up on his chair, tucks his legs to his chest, drops his head back and wonders if anyone will notice if he just climbs under his desk with Benji and spends the day there.

"I'm really not sure anymore."

"Well, I don't know you that well, but I'd wager that you can do better." Benji looks up, smiles in a way that makes Simon's heart trip in his chest. Is he flirting? He's totally flirting.

Simon drops his feet, sets his elbows on the arm rests and stretches his shoulders back, chest puffing out, is pleased to note the way Benji's eyes follow the movement, and oh yes. This could be fun.

"You know what else? I'm not even sure what artisanal really is."

"It's technically traditional foods hand made in small batches, though if you ask me it's been bastardized lately." He unscrews something with his brow furrowed, then clamps the screwdriver between his front teeth. Simon pulls his collar away from his neck, suddenly flushed with warmth.

"Wait. Was that rhetorical?" Benji says around the screwdriver.

"No, I like that answer. Very informative."

Benji looks up with a crooked smile, and Simon should really track down whoever is cranking up the thermostat.

Benji yanks out a very important looking group of wires, holds them dangling in his hands and says, "Anyway, I think it's one of those things people are into just because they think they should be."

He sets the wires by Simon's feet, and Simon stares down at them. "I think you may be right."

Chapter Three

Ask Eros: To Hang Like a Horse. Or Not.

I am 34 and recently divorced. I would like to start dating, and at the encouragement of my friends and family, I have signed up for an online dating site. So far I've gone out on a few dates and I have to say, if this is what dating is like these days, I'd rather be single forever. Now just getting a message from someone interested gives me an extreme sense of dread! Any tips on how to keep pushing myself out there despite terrible dates with no chemistry? I'm running out of time before I'll need to be taken out to pasture!

Dear Hang:

Let's go ahead and put the trip to the glue factory on hold; things are not quite that dire yet. The problem may well be that you're putting too much pressure on yourself. Dating should feel like fun, not a periodontal cleaning. If you aren't having a good time, you are under no obligation to continue dating that person or anyone at all. Is it possible that you really aren't ready yet? It's okay to give yourself some time to heal before you head back into the show ring for another go round. In the meantime, focus on that group of supportive friends and family you've got. Something will happen for you when it's meant to, I promise.

spice *(excerpt)*

* * *

Andrew is on his phone, again, just vague declarations that Simon can barely make out over the pulsing electro-pop and conversations being shouted over it all around them. So far Simon has interacted more with the cute pink-haired waitress about the house "hand-made spiced tomato preserves" that would best suit his oxtail and truffle oil burger.

The table next to theirs is rowdy, probably on their third bottle of wine, and having a much better time than he is. Simon pokes at the rest of his food and seriously considers scooting his chair over the few inches between the tables. Then a text pings.

Tia: Bloody Mary's is lonely without you.

Simon: Does it help that the food is obnoxious and my date is ignoring me?

Tia: NO.

Tia: Do I need to come out there? I've got my nut-crushing stilettos on, ready to go.

The pink-haired waitress comes back with the check, and Andrew finally sets down his phone and takes out his wallet. "Told you this place was great."

Simon dodges an elbow thrown out in full-body laughter from the gentleman to his right, grimaces, "so great," and texts Tia.

Simon: I appreciate it but that won't be necessary. Let's try drinks again tomorrow.

Tia: But the night is still young!

Simon: I know. I think I need to go home and spoon with my dog now.

Andrew gets up, pulls out Simon's chair and helps him into the blazer he insisted Simon borrow. It feels heavy and thick, too much for his smaller build. Andrew guides him out of the restaurant with a hand gripped to his elbow, then a quick kiss outside and he's back on his phone and getting into a cab without a look back at Simon still on the sidewalk.

Tia: I worry about you.

Simon: Can't imagine why. I'll save some doggie kisses for you.

Tia: I'll pass.

Benji is back the next morning, lining up computer parts, installing circuit boards and microchips and whatever the hell else is happening on the floor of Simon's cubicle, and Simon had never realized just how lonely and boring his little blue cubicle was before Benji arrived to dissect his circuit board.

"Favorite cartoon?" Simon asks, continuing their back-and-forth.

"*Ren & Stimpy*." Benji is cross-legged, removing and replacing parts. He's just so sweet, easy to talk to. No bullshit posturing. Today he's wearing a black shirt with narwhals who have lightsabers instead of horns.

"Oh that's a good one. I was gonna say *Sponge Bob* but no, that's better."

"Okay. Best Power Ranger."

"Jason. Red." Simon says without hesitation.

"Over Tommy the sexy smooth green ranger? Come on."

"He had a ponytail," Simon argues.

Benji blinks up at him. "Exactly."

Simon laughs and moves closer, accidentally kicking something that looks sort of important. Benji moves it.

"Favorite Disney movie?"

"Actually," Benji snaps something in place, takes out something else. Simon has given up trying to figure out just what he's doing. "I never really watched them. My older brothers always put on like, *The Terminator* or *Jurassic Park* or *Die Hard*. I never really got a say in movie selection."

"Ah. The benefits of being an only child: I got to watch whatever the hell I wanted to."

Benji hums in agreement and focuses on working, the energy between them settling into a comfortable silence. Simon writes some notes on a yellow legal pad, stealing glances at Benji from time to time. There's something about watching him move so skillfully and confidently. Not just trying to look as though he knows what he's doing, but actually knowing. It's quietly sensual.

"Hey, what are you doing after work?" Simon asks; a sudden uptick in his heart rate surprises him a bit.

"If I say a *Star Wars* marathon at home, will you judge me?" Benji looks up with wide eyes, computer parts scattered around him like a ritual sacrifice to the digital age gods.

Simon turns, opens the decrepit laptop he's being forced to work on for now and starts a blank Word document. "Oh, definitely."

Bloody Mary's is the sort of basement dive bar Simon would have never set foot into if Tia hadn't told him to stop being a slack-jawed tourist of the city and try living in it for real. It's dark and dank, a wooden bar stretched across one end, a scattering of round tables sticky and nicked and marked with rings from thousands of martini glasses and pints of beer.

"Simon!" Tia calls from a green-pleather-topped bar stool as he comes down the stairs, Benji following behind him.

"Hi, you look gorgeous." He kisses her cheek, slides onto the stool next to her. "This is Benji from IT. Which is probably not his full name."

"I know Benji. McGee, right?"

"Close. McHugh." Benji spins a coaster on the bar top. "And you're Tia Robinson of the perpetually slow internet."

Tia sips her drink. "I swear my office has some kind of voodoo hex on it."

"Damn! I was hoping you wouldn't find out about that," Simon says.

Tia scoffs. "Just for that you're buying the next round."

Simon orders. The bartender mixes three whiskey sours with a, "here ya go."

"Play darts with me," Tia sets down her empty glass with a thunk and grabs Simon's hand.

"Since when do you play darts?" Simon asks, pulling a red winged set out from the board, which is riddled with tiny holes.

Tia snags one, throws it in a perfect arc at the board and nearly hits a bullseye. Simon gapes at her. "Since I needed to ask you about the man candy you brought. I didn't know you were into carrot tops."

"I'm not." Simon replies. Takes a dart and misses by a mile. "He's just—nice. I enjoy being around him, and he wasn't doing anything so..." He shrugs.

Tia glances back at the bar, throws another dart that hits just a little farther off. "Good."

One more round and they see Tia off in a cab, home to her fiancé; from the backseat she gives him an eyebrow waggle, which Simon hopes Benji didn't catch. Benji's place turns out to be on the way to Simon's subway stop, so they walk there together in the night that's turning thick with the first humid hint of summer.

"This is me," Benji stops in front of a building, hand in his pocket to get out keys. "I had fun; thanks for inviting me out."

"Yeah, me too."

Then Benji's hand is on his arm, and he looks amazing in the soft light spilling from a street lamp. It would be the easiest thing in the world to just lean in and kiss him. But Simon hesitates too long, unsure of what Benji wants or what he wants, and Benji clears his throat and steps back.

"See you on Monday, Simon."

When he gets home, he's greeted by an enthusiastic Walt and the shredded remains of a boot that must have been left out. Simon cleans it up with a sigh. It's not the first time and it won't be the last, so he tries to not get frustrated. When he's bored, Walt gets into things he shouldn't. Simon has only himself to blame. Maybe doggie day care isn't as ridiculously indulgent as he thought.

Simon finds a rope to play a game of tug of war. A message from Andrew about *doing lunch* pops up on his phone as he sits on the floor and pulls at the rope with both hands.

"Drop it," Simon commands, and Walt does, plopping on his haunches with ears perked and tail whipping back and forth. He throws the rope down the hall, and when Walt charges after it, he reaches to get his phone from the coffee table.

Andrew's text is at the top of his list of messages. Tia next. Mom. After that is a new number, Benji double-checking the time for drinks before they met. Simon presses his lips flat, finger hovering over his options, and types a message.

Simon: I'm thinking about growing a handlebar mustache. Think I can pull it off?

Walt returns with the rope, drops it in Simon's lap and waits.

Benji: Totally. But you should know I have a thing for guys who look like silent film villains.

Simon grins, tucks his phone to his chest and throws the rope again.

interlude **press**

One Story Can Change
Everything.

interludepress.com

Twitter: @interludepress * * * Facebook: Interlude Press
Google+: +interludepress * * * Pinterest: interludepress
Instagram: InterludePress